COMING HOME TO ME THIS CHRISTMAS

CP WARD

"Coming Home to Me This Christmas"
Copyright © CP Ward 2019

The right of Chris Ward to be identified as the Author of this Work has been asserted by him in accordance with the Copyright, Designs and Patents Act 1988.

All rights reserved. No part of this publication may be reproduced, stored in a retrieval system, or transmitted, in any form or by any means without the prior written permission of the Author.

This story is a work of fiction and is a product of the Author's imagination. All resemblances to actual locations or to persons living or dead are entirely coincidental.

BY CP WARD

I'm Glad I Found You This Christmas
We'll have a Wonderful Cornish Christmas
Coming Home to Me This Christmas

COMING HOME TO ME THIS CHRISTMAS

1
WINDING DOWN

Three weeks on the road with her best friend Karen Clarke had been delightful, but Emily Wilson had entered it with a worrying awareness that their trip was temporary, that no matter what adventures they found themselves embroiled in, they would reach a point when they would be looking back, wistful at what had come and gone, with the end tugging at their hard-travelled shoes like the teeth of a hungry dog.

Two days left. Well, one really, when you considered that the last day was a transit day, with perhaps a free hour to walk around Hamburg in the early morning, before heading to the airport and the flight home, back to reality.

And so, technically the second-to-last day had come, but as they sat sipping café lattes on an outdoor terrace by the River Elbe in Hamburg's Blankenese district, they both knew what neither wanted to say, that the end was coming, and the return to shattering reality was imminent.

'It won't be so bad,' Karen said, forest-green roll-neck sweater, sixties-style horn-rimmed glasses and a waterfall of unkempt dark brown hair the very epitome of understated beauty. That she wasn't approached on a daily basis to model raincoats and wellington boots for geeky-yet-gorgeous fashion lines had mystified Emily for years. Karen was as natural a beauty as she had ever known, yet her friend's eternal humility and joy for the simple things in life was as admirable as it was at times frustrating.

Emily nodded. 'I know. Things will work out. Life carries on, doesn't it?'

It was what she was expected to say. Had she cross-referenced the exchange against the circumstances in a social contact textbook, it would have displayed their exact conversation. Sticking to the script was important, because that implied normality, that she had coped, that she continued to cope.

She reached for her latte, but halfway there she felt an attack of the intense sadness that had plagued her over the last two months since her beloved grandmother had passed away. She gripped the edge of the table hard enough to make the fold-out legs tremble against the pavement as though she could hold back the tears she knew were coming.

'I'm sorry,' she gulped, the second syllable jumping out of her mouth like a fish, causing the people on the table beside them to turn around in alarm. Karen soothed them with the kind of calming look her appearance offered as a prerequisite, then she reached across the table and took Emily's hand.

'You're grieving. It's okay. Crying is good. Crying helps.'

Emily felt like an idiot, sobbing in the middle of a busy café. With Karen on hand to offer stability, the other customers gave her just a cursory glance before getting back to their conversations. That was the thing about Karen; she was like a human windbreak, able to halt the tide of calamity in a single look. Had she been bottleable, she would have been worth a fortune.

Emily laughed through the tears until the heaving in her chest eased and she could talk without her words being interspersed with gasps.

'It's nearly over,' she said. 'It was such a great holiday. Thank you so much, Karen. It helped me forget.'

Karen smiled. 'The purpose was not to help you forget, but help you deal with it. I know it's going to be hard, with Christmas coming up, but you know you're welcome at David's place. His parents love you, and they always put on such an event.'

At mention of David, Emily suppressed a groan. Emily had chosen the perfect boyfriend, a man so undislikeable that you wanted to hate him simply for being so nice. Handsome and intelligent, he worked as an artist, but was one of those rare commodities in that he was a successful one. Creative, and also able to make money from it. And his family, whom Emily had met on a number of occasions, were Hallmark perfect. Wealthy upper-class people living in a beautiful country house but almost nauseatingly generous, especially at Christmas time.

After a pause, Emily shook her head. 'I can't,' she said. 'I'd only be a sobbing gooseberry, getting in the way and ruining everyone's Christmas.'

'Don't be ridiculous,' Karen said. 'You know what his parents are like. They don't do intimate Christmases. There'll be at least twenty people there on any given day. All six of David's brothers are coming this year, and since most of them have wives and kids it'll be like living in a rabbit warren. And that's not to mention all David's dishy private school mates who usually show up at some point for sherry or whatever poncey drink the M-I-L has bought in bulk this year.' She leaned forward, lowering her voice. 'You never know, you might meet someone special.'

Emily gave a vehement shake of her head. 'Absolutely not,' she said.

'Why not? David's mates are of a pretty good stock, if you know what I mean. At least a couple of them are single.'

'I'm not looking for a boyfriend,' Emily said. 'I just couldn't handle the stress of it. Not right now.'

'Well, just come and have a laugh, then.'

Emily smiled. 'Thanks to you, I've had all the laughs I could possibly need over the last three weeks. It's been wonderful. For Christmas, though … I think I just need some me time. A few days alone to face up to everything and figure out what I'm going to do next.'

Karen nodded. 'Sure. If that's what you want, but

the offer will always be open. It's not that far. You could just jump on a train, or I suppose now you could afford a taxi.'

Emily gave a wry smile. 'Yeah, or charter a jet.'

'I'm sorry. I know that's part of the problem.'

'In some ways, for sure.'

'You're in a position many people would dream of,' Karen said quietly, as though afraid of making Emily upset. 'I mean, I know you'd give anything to have your grandmother back—'

'In a heartbeat,' Emily said. 'But it is what it is. I have to deal with it.' She shrugged. 'I don't know, perhaps I'll open up the teahouse again. It's just that right now, I can't bring myself to even walk in through the door. The memories, you know?'

Karen nodded. 'Give it time, that's all that I can say.'

Before Emily could respond, Karen reached into her bag and dropped her heavy Germany Lonely Planet Guide on the table. Emily smiled at the doorstop of a book, which Karen had been lugging around in her handbag for their entire trip.

'What does the traveller's bible have to say?' she said.

Karen opened it to a bookmarked page. 'Well, it's our last night, and we agreed to do the Christmas Market this evening. However, we need something to fill the afternoon.'

For three weeks, they had travelled their way around Germany, visiting museums, wandering through castles, drinking in beer halls. It had been the trip of a lifetime, despite the circumstances.

'I'm feeling a bit cultured out, to be honest,' Emily said. 'I've seen enough historical buildings to last a lifetime. Shall we just do a bit of shopping?'

Karen shook her head. 'We can rush-shop tomorrow morning if you like. We'll have a couple of hours before we have to fly. This is our last chance to do something different. Let's see if there's anything interesting that we've missed.'

She leaned over the book, but at that moment a breeze picked up and blew a few pages over. Karen scowled, then went to turn back to the Hamburg section, but as her fingers rested on the paper, she paused.

'Hang on a minute, what's this?'

'What?'

'Oh, this could be interesting.'

'Let me see.'

Karen turned the book around and pointed at a short entry in the *Hamburg & Surrounds* section.

While Emily leaned over the book, Karen pulled a smartphone out of her pocket and started tapping away at the screen. 'Look, I know you're not interested in finding a boyfriend right now, but it could be fun—'

Emily looked up. 'Bridegroom Oak? That just sounds weird.'

'Well, let's find out.' Karen stood up. 'Come on. Our train leaves in fifteen minutes. We'd better get a move on if we're going to get there before dark.'

2
BRIDEGROOM OAK

Until they boarded the train, Karen didn't consider it worth mentioning that the trip to Eutin and the tree known as Bridegroom Oak was rather longer than Emily might have liked for her last day of their holiday. As the train trundled north to Kiel, from where they needed to change for Eutin, Emily had plenty of time to reflect on what had happened over the last few months to bring her here.

Her grandmother, Elaine Margaret Wilson, had passed away on October 1st, at the ripe old age of eighty-seven. She had died happy, in her sleep, after a pleasant evening of dinner and card games with her granddaughter, who had been sleeping in the adjacent room. Emily's shock at finding her grandmother the next morning, seemingly asleep but with a gentle smile on her face, might have been ameliorated by the fact that it was not wholly unexpected; Elaine had been elderly, and by her own admission had not been long for the world.

Really Emily, at the age of twenty-nine, should have been happy that twenty-seven years had passed between the two major tragedies in her life, but it was the ensuing circumstances which continued to cause her the most distress.

'She was my only family,' she said to Karen, sitting across the table from her in the train's buffet car. Karen, as attentive as ever, nodded with understanding, even though she already knew the details so well she could have written the book on Emily's life.

'After my parents died in the crash, she brought me up.' Emily sighed. 'I don't even remember them, even when I see photographs. They're just people, little more than strangers. My grandmother was my whole life.'

With her own husband—Emily's maternal grandfather—having passed away early in life, Elaine had thrown herself into a second parenthood at the age of sixty, bringing Emily up with such ease that Emily considered her a grandmother in name only; Elaine had been father, mother, siblings, best friend, and at times even teacher, all rolled into one. And later, after university, when Emily returned to her home town to help her aging grandmother in her teahouse, Elaine had been manager.

The void her passing left in Emily's life was barely comprehensible.

'What about your grandparents on your dad's side?'

Emily laughed. 'I've met them once, when I was fourteen. They were heading to France in a campervan and they parked in our driveway for a night. After they went off to Europe, I don't think they ever came back. For a few years we got a Christmas card from them, with unusual postmarks—Denmark, Latvia, once even Kazakhstan. The last one came when I was nineteen. I don't know what happened to them after that.'

'And you've got no cousins, have you?'

Emily sighed. 'Both Dad and Mum were only children.' She tried to smile, but the next line came out as barely more than a whisper, as she fought to hold back tears: 'Nope. I'm quite alone in the world.'

Karen patted her hand. 'A good job you've got me.'

Emily wiped away a tear, and was about to say something ridiculously sentimental when an announcement came over the loudspeaker that they were entering Kiel Station.

'This is us,' Karen said. 'Not long to go now.'

After changing to a commuter train, they reached Eutin an hour later. A pretty little town made even prettier by the Christmas tree standing in a square outside the station, and the strings of fairy lights on local businesses, Karen pointed out that they didn't have time to linger if they wanted to get to the Bridegroom Oak before it got dark.

They found a taxi rank outside the station and climbed into the nearest.

'Bridegroom Oak,' Karen told the driver, an elderly German man.

'Ah, you looking for love?' he said with a grin. 'Two pretty girls like you? What the world coming to, eh?'

With another chuckle he pulled them out into traffic, tapping on the wheel in time to a Christmas song playing at low volume on the radio.

'What on earth have you got us into?' Emily whispered.

Karen just smiled. 'You'll see.'

Twenty minutes later, the taxi stopped by the side of the road. They appeared to be in the middle of a small forest, but the driver indicated a wooden sign pointing away into the trees.

'It's that way. If you like, I wait; if not, one mile straight, you find a café.' He handed over a business card. 'You need ride back, you call me.'

'Danke,' Karen said, smiling as she popped the card into her purse.

They paid the driver and got out, giving him a brief wave as the car pulled away. The road was quiet besides a gentle breeze through the trees. Patches of snow lay in some areas alongside the road, and it was cold enough that Emily was glad she had worn a second sweater underneath her jacket.

The sign pointed to a path leading into the trees. Fairy lights had been strung up on either side of the path to illuminate their way through the gloom that had taken over the world outside the sun. Emily glanced at her watch. Three-fifteen. They had about forty-five minutes until dark.

It was a short walk through the forest to the Bridegroom Oak. Emily knew it as soon as she saw it, an ancient tree set apart in a clearing, surrounded by fences to keep people away from its root area, with a single path leading right up to it, a wooden stepladder at the end allowing you to reach a small hole in the trunk, identified by yellow paint around the outside. She already felt intrigued; the fairy lights strung up along the fences only made it seem more magical, like she had stepped through a door into Narnia or Wonderland.

'It's the only tree in the world with its own postal address,' Karen said, her Lonely Planet in hand. 'For more than a hundred years, ever since two lovers used it as a secret meeting place, people have been sending letters to it, hoping to find love.'

'Sounds a bit weird,' Emily said. 'Don't the letters get wet?'

Karen rolled her eyes. 'Apparently not. Even the postman who used to bring the letters found his wife through it,' she said. 'Come on, let's take a look.'

They approached the tree. Karen waved Emily first, but Emily shook her head.

'Go on, it was your idea.'

'I've already got a boyfriend.'

'And I'm not looking. Just have a look.'

'If you insist.'

Karen walked up to the stepladder, tested it for strength, and climbed up. She looked back as she reached the top, then, with the same tentativeness as Flash Gordon putting his hand into the Wood Beast's tree stump, she reached into the hole.

'Wow!' she said. 'There's loads of letters in here.'

'Let's have a look at a few, then.'

Karen withdrew her hand and climbed back down. She passed a couple of envelopes to Emily, then turned over the others in her hand. 'Postmarked Belgium, this one is.'

'And this one is Australia!'

'France.'

'Morocco.'

'Huh. Let's have a look.'

'Why are some of them open?' Emily asked, pulling the letter out.

'That's the rule,' Karen said. 'According to the guidebook, anyone is allowed to visit and open the letters. But you're only allowed to take one if you decide to reply to it.'

'*Kind-hearted, gentle, retiree, looking for a golden-haired golden heart,*' Emily read, then folded the letter back up and slipped it back inside the envelope. 'I don't think that one is quite right.'

'Oh, so you're thinking of replying to one?'

'I didn't say that!'

'Look. This one is from London, and it's still sealed.' Karen opened the letter. '*Help required. An ability with hammer and nails a must to mend a broken heart. I'm forty-five, divorced, but the kids are grown up! Looking for a partner for fun nights in the pub.*'

Emily shrugged. 'I'll pass.'

'Go on, you have a look. Put these back and see what else we can find.'

Emily glanced at her watch. 'It'll be dark soon.'

'Then you'd better hurry up.'

With the letters in hand, Emily climbed up to the hole in the tree. She reached inside, felt a large pile of letters lying inside, dropped the ones she was holding and went to take a few more. The sensation was strange, like she had her hand in a cookie jar, picking something potluck which could lead to an adventure. She reached down farther, enjoying the feel of the envelopes on her fingers, the smooth edges, the rough corners of ones that had been opened and returned, the softness of those touched many times. She reached deeper until her whole arm was inside the tree, then brought up a few that felt cold to the touch.

Dead letters, forgotten.

She climbed back down and passed the letters to Karen.

'Oh, look. China. And this one is from Brazil. Wow, it's been in there four years.' She withdrew the letter. '*My name is Pedro. I'm sixty-seven. I have a small house but a big heart. If you're alone in the world, come and be alone with me in beautiful Sao Paulo.*' She looked up. 'Shall we keep it?'

'He'd be seventy now!'

'Oh, so sixty-seven would be okay?'

Emily chuckled. 'Come on, we'd better go. This was fun, but it's getting dark. I don't fancy walking back through that forest, even with all these fairy lights.'

Karen sighed. 'Okay, I suppose you're right. Oh,

look. This is another one from England. Cottonwood. Isn't that near you?'

'Oh my God, it is. Let me see.'

Emily took the letter and opened it. Written on a ragged piece of notepaper that had been torn off a telephone pad, it had the watermark for an insurance company at the top.

Dear Tree,
  I'm looking for someone to save Christmas.
  Asking for a friend. Actually, several.

At the bottom was a return post office address.

'What does it say?' Karen said, leaning closer.

'That's all,' Emily said.

'Might be a joke.'

Emily shrugged. 'It doesn't sound like it.' She turned the envelope over. 'It's postmarked last year, so it doesn't look like his wish was ever granted.'

'Well, I suppose we'd better go.' Karen grinned. 'Are you sure you don't want that one from Brazil? I've seen pictures of the beaches in Sao Paulo. They're really nice.'

'I'll pass, but thanks.'

Emily took the letters from Karen, climbed up the tree and slid them back inside. As she heard the rustle of them landing, she felt a sudden lurching sense of regret. For a few seconds she stood, her fingers on the trunk of the ancient oak, just listening to the sound of the forest, of the wind in the trees.

With a shrug, she turned away.

They headed back along the path, but had gone no more than halfway when Emily stopped.

'What is it?' Karen asked.

'I, um … nature calls.'

'What, right now?'

'Yeah.'

'The taxi driver said there was a café just up the road. Can't you wait until then?'

'Um, no.'

'Well, go on then. I'll turn around.'

'You wait here. I'll go back by the tree.'

'What, and leave me here?'

'You'll be in earshot. Keep talking to me. I'll just find a quiet place. Shout if someone comes along.'

'Just hurry up.'

Emily turned and hurried back along the path. She didn't understand why her heart was beating so hard, but as the tree came into view it began to thunder as though she had just run a marathon. She ran to the stepladder and climbed up, reaching quickly inside.

There had to be a hundred letters piled up in the hollow inside the tree's trunk. Emily pulled a handful out and flicked through them, but recognised none. She put them back inside, then pulled out another handful. Where was it…?

'Come on, Emily!' came Karen's voice from back through the trees. 'Your bum must be freezing by now!'

Suppressing a smile that did nothing to alleviate her growing frustration, Emily thrust her hand back inside once more. If she didn't find it this time, she would give up.

She pulled a handful of letters out, flicking through them.

There.

Postmarked Exeter, a return address in Cottonwood.

She unzipped her jacket and slipped the letter into an inside pocket.

It might be nothing.

It probably was nothing.

Nothing at all.

Certainly not.

When she got back to Karen a couple of minutes later, her friend lifted an eyebrow.

'You took your time,' she said. 'Anyone would think you went back to get a letter.'

Emily shrugged. 'I was cold, that was all. Nature took a little longer to call than I expected.'

3

MEMORIES

THE SIGN IN THE WINDOW SAID CLOSED UNTIL FURTHER NOTICE. Emily pulled her key out of her pocket and unlocked the teahouse door, stepping over a pile of mail on the mat inside.

She put down her bag on a table just inside the entrance before leaning down to pick up the bundle of letters and leaflets. Most of it was circulars, but she also found a couple of bills and one or two legal letters no doubt following up on her grandmother's estate arrangements. Most heartbreaking of all, however, were the dozen or so Christmas cards at the bottom. It was only December tenth, but Elaine had been popular. They had always enjoyed counting them each Christmas, then tying them up on strings and hanging them around the teahouse until they created a decorative wall of miniature North Poles, red-chested robins, Father Christmases, and tiny nativities. Two hundred and twelve, that had been their seasonal record, the last Christmas just gone.

That was the thing about Emily's grandmother. Even as she got older, she had only become more popular.

Emily put the cards down on the table and went through an internal door into the main café area. To the left, the tables and chairs were still set up in readiness beneath the glass conservatory roof. Shadows mottled many of the tables, Emily saw, and she glanced up to see leaves scattered over the glass, something her grandmother had never allowed. One of Emily's jobs each morning had been to get up on the stepladder and clear the leaves with an ancient, heavy leaf-blower that dated back to the early eighties. It was a relic of the grandfather Emily had never known, one of numerous ancient gardening tools and machines which populated the adjoining house, rear garage, and garden shed like abandoned robots waiting for a chance to come back to life.

She continued inside, past the serving counter with its empty glass cabinets once filled with pastries, fresh sandwiches, and homemade scones, now sprinkled with a grey dust layer. Into the teahouse kitchen, all government-regulation stainless steel but with her grandmother's touch: frilled curtains, posies of dried flowers hanging from the wall, small animal figurines along each shelf.

Untouched since the day Elaine had died, a vase that had once been filled with bright flowers was now dry, the flowers reduced to blackened stalks which had flaked over the windowsill below. Emily, who had barely been able to enter the teahouse over the last couple of months, took the vase and emptied the remains of the flowers into a bin. Replacing the vase on the table, she retreated to the door, looking back into the main hall and through the conservatory doors onto a patio terrace with views stretching down across her grandmother's garden then across fields and patches of forest toward Dartmoor rising in the distance.

Over the first few days, local people, who had made up the bread and butter around the waves of tourists who had come from far and wide to enjoy her grandmother's famous cakes, had often stopped by to wish Emily well, offer condolences, and politely enquire about when the teahouse might reopen. Emily, still in the worst stages of her grief, had brushed them off as best she could, but as days turned into weeks she had found the only thing she could do was put a sign in the window and cancel all upcoming deliveries.

Of course, there had been other problems, that Emily, in her years of blissful innocence as her grandmother's assistant, had failed to anticipate. Even into her eighties, Elaine had been business-savvy, setting up a website to take advance bookings, which Emily had only discovered when the first people began to show up, creating much confusion. Now replaced with a temporary notification of a site under maintenance, at least people weren't showing up unannounced anymore, but Emily had further problems.

The teahouse had been her grandmother's life for over thirty-five years, a project to pour her love into after her beloved husband had died in early middle-age. And she had been successful: even on the darkest, rainiest days of the off-season, people had still come through the doors, and on busy summer days, or during the frequent special events her grandmother had so excelled in, there had rarely been a table free. As recently as the summer just gone, Elaine had been talking about extending the outside terrace to allow extra tables.

Now, the doors closed, the orders cancelled, the website down and the part-time staff requested to look for new positions, the teahouse had become a shadow. Emily knew what her grandmother would have wanted, but here in this place where the old woman had been so alive, Emily found life unbearable without her.

The tears were coming. She went out of the teahouse, through a door marked PRIVATE, and into the two-storey connected cottage they had always shared. Here, at least, she had begun to move on. She had sorted through some of her grandmother's clothes, assessing what she could give to charity and what was best for the bin. In a couple of extra rooms used only for junk, she had begun to pick through boxes, tossing away bags of ancient, dog-eared electric, water, and phone bills, old documents and magazines which her grandmother—a natural hoarder—had kept not through sentiment but through routine.

Standing at the bottom of the stairs, she was just deliberating whether to go into the garden and maybe rake up some leaves, or go upstairs and get straight into clearing out some junk, when her phone rang.

'Are you all right over there?' came Karen's voice.

'I kept checking my watch. I guessed you've been home about twenty minutes, and the sentimentality is starting to get to you, am I right?'

Emily laughed, a sound her grandmother would have approved of, even in these desperate times.

'Have you installed me with a spy camera?'

'No, I just know you. You're not the type to stop by Sainsbury's on the way home. You're a straight home, cup of tea kind of girl.'

'I haven't made the tea yet.'

'But you would have done before you did anything productive.'

Emily nodded. 'You're right. I would have. I was just deciding what to do.'

'Come and stay with me,' Karen said. 'I know we've only just got back, but we're into that holiday hangover stage, and in your circumstances, yours will be worse than any other. I'm worried about you being on your own over there.'

Karen only lived a twenty-minute drive away, but Emily shook her head. 'I have to deal with it,' she said. 'I've been running away, trying to avoid it all. It's just hard, you know. This place was everything to her. I can never replace her, and it wouldn't be right to try.'

'Perhaps leave it a while, then.'

Emily grimaced. 'Christmas was her favourite time of the year. She used to turn the teahouse into a grotto, and the whole garden became a Christmas illumination scene. I know I should open up in her memory, it's just … you know.'

'Without her, it doesn't feel right.'

'Exactly.'

'Perhaps take this Christmas off, then.'

Emily nodded. 'I have to pull myself together, I know. I can't go on like this. It's just, the healing process, I didn't think it would take this long.'

'Everyone grieves in a different way,' Karen said. 'Just give it time. Don't make any big decisions until your head is clear. It sounds like you still need to get out of there. You know, the offer to come down to David's is still open.'

'I know. I'll think about it.'

'We're all heading over there on the fifteenth and staying until the fourth. You won't be a gooseberry, I promise. There'll be twenty people there at least.'

'I think about it, that's all I can say.'

Karen went quiet for a moment. 'Are you thinking about Cottonwood?'

'What?'

'I know you took that letter.'

'I—what? I don't know what you mean.'

Karen laughed. 'It was poking out of your jacket pocket. Are you going to go over there and see what it was about?'

Emily groaned. 'Oh, that was a silly, childish whim. I mean, it was probably only sent as a joke. And it was sent last year. I imagine it's a bit late by now.'

'But it was never answered, because the letter was still there. They could still be waiting for someone to come and save their Christmas.'

'Are you mocking me?'

'Of course not. But if you're going to drive down

there, perhaps hunt out a Father Christmas suit before you go.'

'It's not funny.'

'I know; just trying to make you smile.'

'I am smiling.'

'Well, that's good then. Seriously, are you going to go over there?'

Emily considered. She hadn't had time to read over the letter since her return, but it would be a lie to say she hadn't thought about it. In fact, she had thought about it a lot. Whether she was someone who could make a difference or not, she didn't know, but if nothing else it had got her intrigued. Unsigned, the letter and its reasoning had caught her imagination and was nagging at her like a frustrated child. Cottonwood was barely half an hour away by car; it wouldn't hurt just to drive over and have a look around, maybe ask a few questions.

'You're wondering if you've got enough petrol in the car, aren't you?' Karen said, voice barely more than whisper.

'No,' Emily said. 'I filled up on the way down.'

4
COTTONWOOD

She had seen it on a map, of course, but never had cause to come here. Hidden down the country lanes tangled between two major roads, it was one of those places which everyone local knew of, but, unless you had a relative living there, you had little reason to pass through. As a result, after passing a sign saying "Welcome to Cottonwood", Emily found herself surprised to discover that rather than a collection of isolated houses as she had expected, Cottonwood was actually a genuine village. A neat flowerbed-lined green stood at its centre, overlooked by a church on one side of the triangular village square, a pub on the left, and a terrace of holiday lets on the right. Three narrow roads led off. Initially lined with houses, they eventually turned into farmland. As she pulled into a parking space marked in gravel outside the church, Emily counted three shops tucked in between the houses: one general store and post office, one for gardening supplies, and a third which appeared to be half bookshop, half cafe. Three empty tables stood outside with menus stabbed into plastic holders waving in the breeze.

The first thought that came to mind was how quiet the place was. A couple of other cars were parked outside the church and a few more lined the streets, but there was no sign of any people.

Emily climbed out. She glanced at her watch, finding it was just after two p.m. It was Tuesday, so many people would still be at work. For mid-December, the weather was remarkably warm, even as a breeze rattled along the street to the south, hassling her from behind.

Emily, initially in a dark blue sweater, took a light jacket out of the back of her car and zipped it up in front, before taking a quick circle of the square to see what was around. It appeared that the village petered out quite quickly down two of its three intersecting roads, although the third—the way she had come in—extended into a wider residential area containing a few small cul-de-sacs and more modern estate houses. She took the branch to heading right past the church just to see where it went, and within a couple of hundred metres she had passed the last of the houses and found herself walking along tall hedges blocking a view of rolling farmland occasionally glimpsed through open gateways. Backtracking, she found that the left-hand road was much the same, but the road she had come in by had a few small commercial properties hidden among the residential, including a couple of cafés and a small art supplies shop. Even so,

Cottonwood had to number no more than a hundred buildings.

With a wry smile, she realised she could probably establish the writer of the Bridegroom Oak's letter simply with an afternoon of door-knocking.

Still, cold calling wasn't her speciality, so she chose the next best option and headed for the pub.

A heavy oak door creaked as she entered. She found herself in a gloomy, low-ceilinged room with a bar at one end, three tables set along the outer wall to her left, and a tired, grimy pool table in the middle.

'Shut at three,' came a voice from behind the bar, and it took Emily a moment to notice an old man sitting on a bar stool in the corner, a newspaper open in front of him. 'Food's stopped serving—six months ago, actually—but I can get you a drink.'

Emily's first instinct was to turn and run, escape from the confines of the unhappy bar back out into the warm sunshine, but the questions were starting to queue up. Emily, who had planned to pretend Christmas didn't exist, wondered why this pub—surely with money to be made—was doing the same.

'Merry Christmas,' she said, coming closer, halfway down the bar, close enough to get a good look at the man but far enough away to make a break for the door if necessary. 'I'll have a coffee, if you've got one. And a packet of crisps?'

The man stood up, giving his back a quick rub as he did so. Emily could almost hear his bones creak as he made his way behind the bar to a coffee machine at the far end.

'I'm afraid the filter's been on all morning,' he

said, holding up a bulbous glass jug with a depressing puddle of tar-like liquid at the bottom. 'I can do you an instant, if you like. Got some Tesco stuff that's not half bad.'

Emily smiled. 'That would be great.'

The man sighed as he set a kettle to boil then leaned down to retrieve a half-full bottle of milk out of the fridge. Emily lifted an eyebrow at the kind of bottle that had gone out of fashion with milk rounds twenty years ago. She remembered her grandmother ordering in a crate every day, 'because it tastes better.' A five-year-old Emily had always loved picking off the aluminium lids and spooning out the cream, which Elaine had used as an ingredient in some of her cakes. Her grandmother always said they lost something of their kick after the milk round to their village closed down in 1995, and they were forced to buy cartons like everyone else.

'Why the smile?' the man asked, offering one of his own. 'A bit early in the day for that.'

Emily shrugged. 'I was just remembering something.'

The man followed her gaze and glanced down at the milk bottle. 'Oh, these? Alan, down at Rowe Farm. Does them wholesale.' He chuckled. 'Fresh out of the cow, more or less.'

'It's very … quaint.'

'Isn't it just? You're not from round here, are you? Staying in one of those lets?'

Emily shook her head. 'Just passing through. My name's Emily Wilson. I'm from Birchtide, just outside Exeter.'

'Seen it on the map,' the man said. 'Well, welcome to the Inn on the Green. You can call me Skip. The locals all do. I used to own a boat.'

'Used to?'

'Rower. Got too old to be hauling that thing up and down the river. It's out the back. Kids' sandpit.'

Emily smiled. As Skip said it, she noticed a door to the side of the bar, a small metal sign embedded into the wood saying "Dining Room & Beer Garden".

'That must be fun for them.'

Skip shrugged. 'If anyone ever used it. I go out there every few months and pull up the weeds.' With another sigh, he passed the coffee across the bar. 'Here you are. Need sugar, let me know.'

Emily took a sip. 'Perfect. Like my … grandmother used to make it.'

Skip, clearly in need of conversation, leaned on the bar. Up close, he looked like a stereotypical lifelong landlord with his beer gut, broad shoulders, and skin that could do with more fresh air and less poison. His eyes were rheumy and more hair sprouted from his ears than the top of his head, but when he smiled he had a warmth to him which put Emily at ease, as though the art of casual conversation was a skill he had mastered over long hours propping up the end of the bar.

'So, what brings a young lady like you passing through a place like this? I don't even get the locals passing through much anymore. And those lets have been empty since September.'

Emily felt a sudden reluctance to mention the

letter. It was a fairy story, yet here she was, grounded back in reality. What if Skip laughed?

'I was just out for a drive,' she said. 'I realised I'd never been to Cottonwood, so thought I'd drive through and take a look.'

'Don't you have a job?'

Emily hesitated. 'I'm on holiday,' she said.

'Well, nice for some. Although I might as well be, scant number of folks who come in this place. Had to lay off the cooking staff. Do it all myself now, and no one wants me handling their pies.'

'Won't you get a Christmas rush?' Emily asked. 'I mean, it's only a few days away now. Shouldn't you have a tree or some lights up or something?'

Skip lifted an eyebrow then gave another customary sigh. 'Well, I suppose I could. Got a box of stuff out the back. Not much point now that the parish council's gone and shut everything down, though, is there?'

5
SENTIMENTS

Skip, after settling into a twenty-minute monologue about country life, suddenly announced it was time he should start clearing up, and Emily took her cue to leave. She wasn't sad to see the sun again, but old Skip had been welcome if grizzled company, and Emily, who was used to being on the other side of the conversation, had enjoyed being the customer for a change. Elaine had never tired of dispensing local information, but it had grated on Emily at times. She had questioned why her grandmother hadn't simply handed the customer a flyer for a local attraction instead of giving them a personal account, but it was just that, Elaine had explained, that they wanted: a touch of humanity in a world which was moving away from it.

At just after three, Emily only had an hour or so of daylight left, so she took a walk around the churchyard. Pondering the ancient, listing graves, she was enjoying the calm and quiet, but when she came to a line of newer ones the reality of her life began to return. She bent down to read them, wondering who else might be suffering the same juddering shock of grief that she was.

> *Philip Benjamin Dent*
> *1961-2014*
> *Always in our thoughts*

Fifty-three. It was nothing. Could have been illness, or an accident. She looked at the next, and a tear sprang to her eye.

> *Marjorie Ann Avery*
> *1921-2007*
> *the best sister, mother, wife, and grandmother*
> *ever sent to earth*
> *and a mighty fine cook too*

She couldn't help but laugh at the last line. Eighty-six, almost her grandmother's age. A fine, long life, something she kept trying to remember. Elaine had done good, and died with dignity. Emily knew she should be celebrating her grandmother's life, but all she could see was the void left behind. She moved along to the next.

> *Katherine Susan Rowe*
> *1985-2018*
> *Loving wife to Alan and mother to John and Lily*
> *Taken too soon*
> *Forever in our hearts*

The farmer Skip had mentioned. His wife had died just two years ago at the age of thirty-three. Emily was only twenty-nine; the thought of dying in four short years filled her with dread. It was far too young to be leaving the world, and the children left behind were now without a mother.

The sadness was too much for Emily to bear. Beating a quick retreat, she fled the churchyard and returned to her car.

She sat in the car for a long time before she could do anything. The grief she had hoped to ameliorate by looking at the graves had only returned worse than before. It had been a mistake coming here, she realised now. She was chasing some sort of fantasy which could only have proven a disappointment.

In the end, unable to think of anything else to do, she called Karen.

'Hi, you all right?'

'Do I sound it?'

'You're either drunk or you've been crying, and since you can't take a drink at the best of times, much less at four o'clock on a Tuesday, I'd say the latter.'

'I know it's silly, but—'

'You don't have to explain it. I understand. It's not something you can put a time limit on. Look, the offer's still there, as always. Come up to David's place over Christmas. If you're not opening the teahouse you'll be kicking your heels all day and night, and that's no way to behave, is it?'

'I'll think about it.' She found a tissue in her jacket pocket and sniffed into it.

'Are you at the shop now?'

'No, I'm … I went for a drive.'

A pause. 'Did you now? Let me guess, to a little village which begins with C, is something you use to make clothes, and ends with a little bunch of trees?'

Emily gave a weepy laugh. 'Yeah.'

'And did you find him?'

'Who?'

'The person who wrote that letter?'

'Not yet. I've only been here half an hour.'

'Well, where did you look?'

'Just the pub.'

'There's a surprise.' Karen chuckled. 'Well, what's it like?'

'The pub? Dingy—'

'The village. I've never been there. Is it all magical and Christmassy with fairy lights everywhere?'

'The letter asked for someone to bring Christmas back.'

'So that's a no?'

'No.'

'Well, I suppose that means it hasn't been answered yet. What is it like?'

Emily peered out of the window. A light rain had begun to fall, covering everything with a layer of grey. Behind a rusting fence, the overgrown churchyard hid the path up to the building. Behind her, the grass on the small green was long overdue a cut. A couple of obvious potholes rendered the approach road treacherous, and the few buildings she could see were shabby, the paint peeling, front gardens untended, neglected.

Were it not for the few cars parked nearby,

Cottonwood could have been abandoned, a lost village in the middle of the countryside, its life squeezed out by the duel carriageways on either side. But—

Emily smiled, her eyes glazing over as a sudden image filled her mind. 'Well, with a lick of paint here and there and a bit of work with some shears, plus a bag or two of gravel … oh, and a couple of boxes of fairy lights and a quaint but not intrusively sized tree … I think it could look rather nice.'

Karen laughed. 'It sounds like you're smitten.'

As though breaking out of a daydream, Emily shook her head. 'Well, it was just a fanciful idea. I don't think anything would come of it.'

'Why not?'

'Because it would be too much work. I'd have to pull people together, get them organised, get everything arranged, and there really is no time.'

'You know snow is forecast for next week, don't you?'

'Is it really?'

'Yes. I just saw it on the TV today. Several inches. They reckon we have a white Christmas coming.'

Emily gave a small nod. 'Right then. Well, I suppose there's no time to lose, is there? There's a Christmas which needs to be saved.'

'Good luck. Keep me posted!'

'I will.'

But as Emily hung up and took a deep breath as she peered out into rain that was falling really quite heavily now as the sun dipped behind the hills, she wondered what exactly it was she had agreed to.

6

UPROOTING

During the drive back to Birchtide, Emily's mind was awash with ideas. As she pulled up into her parking space in the teahouse's empty car park, however, she felt doused with a sudden shock of cold water.

The rain had followed her north, and a deluge awaited her as she climbed out of the car and dashed across the sodden gravel car park to the overhang of the teahouse's front entrance. Twilight had fallen, and the sensor-operated outdoor light, gone grubby over three months of neglect, emitted only a dim glow to help her retrieve her door key from her purse.

As Emily stared at it, she realised she didn't want to go inside. This place, which had been her safe haven for as long as she could remember, now seemed dark and unwelcoming. She could barely take a step without meeting a memory of one kind or another: the crack in the ceramic plant pot to the door's left, caused when she had fallen and struck her knee on it aged seven; the heavy fluff of the postbox which had done its best concertina on her university application response letter, leaving her a frantic extra day of waiting before the following day's pizza flyers had pushed it free and sent it tumbling aerodynamically to the floor; the little table with the doily and the pot of plastic flowers where one morning she had found a car key which didn't resemble her grandmother's car key, and was in fact the key for a little mini parked out the front which had been Emily's eighteenth birthday present. Her grandmother, aware of Emily's need for street cred, had made sure to buy something a little bit rusted, a little bit banged up, and with a ripped Kenwood sticker across the back window. Emily had been so happy she had cried so much the first time she took it for a drive that she'd pulled over on three separate occasions.

'Home,' she muttered, only now it was anything but; it was an empty shell stolen of its glorious life force and subsisting only on past glories. An empty shell, the outer wrapper of a discarded box of chocolates, its glorious excitement long faded. Emily had thought she loved this place, but what she realised now was that she had loved what made it special: her grandmother. And without Elaine's cheerful voice and constant hustle and bustle, Emily felt like a stranger.

She went straight upstairs to pack a bag.

Returning downstairs a few minutes later with a bag containing most of the clothes—now washed and dried—which she had packed for Germany, she found the postman had been. Another twenty unopened Christmas cards lay in a neatly fanned circle. Emily scooped them up and slipped them into a side pocket on her bag, along with a couple of pizza delivery circulars, which until her grandmother's death had been unnecessary and unwanted. A firm believer in home-cooked food, Emily had never eaten anything at home which hadn't been produced on Elaine's immaculately clean stove, saving her forays into the world of fast food for rare nights out with her friends. Since Elaine's death, though, she had eaten very little else, and her waistline had begun to suffer. A couple of weeks of trudging around German forests had helped, but with Christmas on the horizon, things were likely to take another turn for the worse. However, home-cooking was something they had always done together, and preparing food alone only brought more nostalgic memories.

Pizza it would have to be, then. Until the New Year, at least. Things would sort themselves out then, Emily hoped.

Either that or she would meat feast herself to death.

She put her bag into the car and set off, but as she reached the turning out of the car park she saw an old couple making their way up the road. The woman lifted a hand to greet her, and Emily reluctantly wound down the window.

Jane and Bert Thomas, two locals and former customers. Since her grandmother's death, Emily had avoided the locals as though the village was infected with a zombie plague and she was the only survivor, but she couldn't just speed past. She offered her best smile as they approached.

'Emily, dear, how are you coping?'

Emily shook her head. 'It's tough, but I'm doing my best.'

'Any news on when the teahouse will be opening up again?'

Emily grimaced. 'I don't know. Right now I'm still dealing with a few things.'

'It must be hard, what you're going through, but it's what your grandmother would have wanted.'

'Why don't you sell up?' Bert said. 'Business like that shouldn't be left fallow.'

'Don't be silly, you old fool,' Jane admonished him. 'She couldn't do that. Elaine would turn in her grave.'

No pressure. 'I haven't made any decisions yet,' Emily said.

'Well, when you do decide to open up again, there'll be a queue at the door.'

'If we've not all died of starvation first,' Bert added, receiving another stern look from his wife.

'Bert, this isn't a time for death jokes.'

'Thought old Elaine's millionaire's shortcake was my death coming,' Bert said. 'As good a way to go out as any.'

'You see?' Jane said to Emily, offering a smile which was supposed to be reassuring. 'Poor Bert's on his last legs. It's what Elaine would have wanted, you know.'

Elaine wanted to live forever, Emily was tempted to say. *We don't always get what we want in life.* Instead, all she said was, 'I'm still sorting through a few things.'

'Of course, dear. We'll be ready when you are.

Where are you off to, anyway?'

Emily suppressed a groan. 'Um, shopping,' she said, which, in a sense, wasn't entirely false.

'Well, you have a good time.'

Emily forced a smile as the Thomases stepped back to let her drive on. She glanced back at them in the mirror as she headed up the street, and saw Jane's walking stick waving dramatically in the direction of the teahouse.

She was letting people down, of course she was. But just for once, she wanted to make her own choice, to do what she wanted to do, rather than what was expected of her.

~

As she had guessed, the three holiday lets in Cottonwood were vacant. Emily found all three on the Airbnb website and booked the middle one. It was overpriced, she thought, but it wasn't like she had any worries about money. She reserved for the next two weeks, comprising the full Christmas period. Then, after a quick stop for petrol and a few toiletries, she headed for her holiday home.

It was fully dark when she arrived, parking in a space outside the church she saw now was reserved for the lets. The residences on either side were still dark and unoccupied, but a downstairs light was on inside the one she had reserved.

Pulling her small suitcase through the potholes behind her, she walked up the cobblestone path to the door and knocked.

She had expected an old woman, or at least someone a little frumpy who might have changed bed linen for a living. The absolute last person she was expecting to open the door was a tall, well built man in his early thirties who could have stepped straight out of a fashion catalogue. Emily was so taken in by the dark eyes, strong jaw, and perfect wave of dark brown hair that would have fallen tidy in a hurricane, that she didn't even realise he had asked a question.

'You're Emily Wilson? You, uh, didn't say anything about disabilities.'

'Huh? What?'

'Your hearing.' He chuckled. 'Is it a problem?'

'Um, say again?' She forced a smile, trying to make a joke but already feeling her cheeks redden. It had been years since a man had left her starstruck, perhaps not since secondary school. She'd had a handful of short-term boyfriends over the years, but none of them had measured up to the stature and sheer poise of the man blocking the entrance to her holiday let.

It was like a Christmas present come early.

'My name's Nathan,' he said. 'I'm the owner of these properties. I have to say, your booking took me by surprise. It was what, an hour ago?'

Emily glanced at her watch. 'Forty-five minutes,' she said. 'Sorry about that. I can be a bit … impulsive.'

The moment the word was out of her mouth, her cheeks began to redden. She might as well have just invited him up to the bed he had probably just made. *I'm supposed to be grieving*, she reminded herself.

'It's fine, don't worry. I forget these places are still on some of those sites. I meant to delist them, but no one ever books them, so I must have forgotten. Well, I guess it's up to you if you really want to spend your Christmas somewhere like Cottonwood.'

'It's charming,' she said. 'And this place looked lovely.'

'Well, if you think so. Shall I show you around?' Nathan asked.

'Yes, please.'

'This way, then.' Nathan led her inside, through a narrow hallway to a quaint kitchen which had a window looking out onto a patio. 'Garden out the back,' Nathan said, switching on a rear outdoor light which briefly illuminated a neat rectangle of grass with a line of rose bushes at the end, before he abruptly switched it off again.

'Take a look through the cupboards, and if there's anything you need which you can't find, give me a call.' He tapped a piece of paper taped to the fridge. 'Contact details. Before nine, please, otherwise the dogs will go mental when the phone rings and annoy the old bag next door.' He smiled, but it was mirthless. She wondered if he was being sarcastic, or whether he really did live next door to someone who liked to cause him trouble.

'Great, thanks.'

Nathan eased past her, out into the hall. He opened a side door and switched on a light. 'Living room,' he said, then pulled the door shut before Emily could get a good look. She was thinking to look for herself but Nathan was already heading up the stairs, waving for her to follow. He reached the landing and switched on a light.

'Bathroom and toilet through there. Bedroom on the left. Any sheets you want changed, there's a bag behind the door with instructions. Leave them out the front and I'll have Audrey come and deal with them.'

'Audrey?'

'She's my regular cleaner. She'll leave them outside the front. I'm afraid you'll have to make the beds up again yourself. After all, this isn't the Ritz.'

'Well, I'm sure that won't be a problem.'

Nathan clapped his hands together. 'Then we're all sorted. I'm afraid that there isn't much in the way of shops in this grotty little place, so if you want my advice, I'd get a lot of use out of your car. Heaven knows what'll happen if we get snowed in next week.'

'Okay, great.'

Nathan eased past her again and made his way down the stairs. At the front door, he turned back. Emily felt her knees weaken. From her vantage point at the top of the stairs looking down, Nathan was hopelessly attractive, his face like a thousand classic movie rogues all rolled into one.

'If you need anything, just call.'

Emily nodded. 'Sure.'

'Enjoy your stay.'

Nathan let himself out. Emily stared at the back of the closing door for a few seconds before the brain haze that had descended on her began to clear. Well, that was a turn up she hadn't expected. Too bad he hadn't been a little bit more positive, but you couldn't ask for everything.

7

VERONICA

It didn't take long to unpack her stuff. There were actually two bedrooms upstairs, but only one had been made up. It had a view down into the street and of the green with the church on the other side. A single light shone outside the church porch, while the square and the three connecting roads were lit by a handful of street lights. The brightest place in the village was the pub, which had lights shining through its windows even though no one could be seen inside. It was fully dark outside, but Emily had to keep reminding herself that it wasn't even dinner time yet.

Dinner.

She had picked up a couple of packets of pasta and some Bolognese mix in the petrol station shop, and she had her takeaway flyers, of course. She also had her car if she wanted to drive anywhere. Nathan had been pretty negative about what could be found around the village, but perhaps he was just a jaded local. It happened sometimes, if you lived too long in the same place and things weren't going the way you might have hoped. Until Elaine's death, Birchtide had seemed an idyllic little place, but now Emily felt penned in, trapped, like a fly stuck in a web.

She finished unpacking her stuff, then went back downstairs and put on her shoes. Outside, a chilly wind was whistling through the streets, seeming to come up from the street to her back, down the one ahead to the left, before wrapping around the church and assaulting her from the front. With the street lights petering out at the end of each line of houses, leaving only a black wall of darkness, she felt cut off from the rest of the world. Only when a Range Rover came bumping down the street to the right, lights on full beam nearly blinding her, was she reminded that there was a way of escape.

The grocery shop a couple of doors from the pub was shut. A sign in its window gave opening times of nine a.m. to four thirty. Back up the street, the little art supplies shop was also shut, even though a sign in the window said it was open until six. Still thinking it was too early for the pub, Emily remembered the third commercial property she had seen, the little bookshop and café, back up the road behind her.

The road arched around to the left, while on the right there was a gap between houses for a field which sloped away into a valley, leaving a view of twinkling lights scattered across distant hillsides. She checked her direction, wondering if the small cluster in the far distance might be Birchtide's small estate, but she couldn't be sure.

Up around the corner on the left, she found the

place she sought still open. The tables out the front had been put away, but through the windows she saw other tables inside, in a clear space beside which was a section of shelves.

'Are you still open?' she called, pushing through the door.

'I suppose,' came a voice from out of sight around a corner. 'What you after?'

A sassy-looking girl of about eighteen sauntered into view. Emily was immediately struck by how different this girl was to her own eighteen-year-old self: hair with tinted highlights was plaited into two antennae-like pinnacles held in place by a series of knitting needles. She wore a Glastonbury t-shirt under an apron decorated with farm animals, and as she put a hand on the counter in front of her, multiple rings glittered on her fingers. At the same age, Emily, in comparison, had been Sandy from the first half of *Grease*.

'Well, I suppose … dinner?'

The girl scoffed. 'Where do you think you are, TGI Fridays? Look, I can heat you up a sausage roll, if that's okay. It'll be from frozen, though. You're my first customer today, apart from Skip, the pub landlord, who came over to grab a few free books.'

'Oh, right. Well, sorry about that. I just arrived.'

The girl shrugged. 'Arrived where? Here? Did you get lost? If you take the left-hand road by the church and keep going, it comes out on the A30.'

'No, I mean I'm staying here.'

'In Cottonwood?'

'Yes.'

'Why?'

Emily paused. Because of the letter? Was that really it? She only lived a few minutes away by road. Was she running away from something?

'I needed to escape,' she said.

'Are you on the run?'

Emily laughed. 'No, of course not. Not that I'm aware of at any rate.'

The girl didn't laugh at the attempted joke. 'Well, I hope not. Shall I get that sausage roll on defrost, then?'

'Sure.'

'Sit wherever you like.'

There were three tables, each adorned with a plain plastic tablecloth, salt and pepper shakers, and a box of napkins. As she sat down, Emily picked up a menu and browsed the list. The first five items were crossed out, leaving only three options: sausage rolls, pasties, and cream teas. A drinks menu also had the first three items crossed out. A line drawn through "filter coffee" had been replaced by "instant".

'You want a drink?' the girl said, leaning over the counter as the sound of a microwave started up behind her. 'I got tea. Run out of sugar, though.'

'No sugar is fine.'

'Also run out of milk.'

'Okay, well, black will be fine.'

'Sure.' The girl cracked her first attempt at a smile. 'Feel free to have a look at the books. They're not for sale, but if you promise to bring them back, you can borrow whatever.'

Emily looked around. The haphazard collection

wouldn't have looked out of place in a charity shop. Broken-spined Stephen Kings were stacked on top of Dean Koontzs and John Grishams. In one corner a box held tatty children's books. Another had oversized coffee table picture books. On the fiction shelves, however, the books had been stuffed wherever they would fit, a romance here, a fantasy there. A Booker Prize winner jammed in next to a Harry Potter.

'Quite a collection,' Emily said.

'Yeah. Was my idea. Thought it might get a few more customers in. Mum wasn't so keen, but whatever.'

The girl emerged from behind the counter carrying a sausage roll on a plate. It had been hopelessly over-microwaved, sagging in the middle where the puff pastry had deflated, the lack of a serviette placed underneath meaning it had likely glued itself to the plate. A sprig of optimistic parsley had been placed on one side. Emily forced a smile.

'Looks delicious.'

'Thanks. You want tomato sauce? I've got a bit left, but I've run out of brown. Been meaning to get to Tesco but my car's got a problem with the gear box and I ain't getting on the bus.'

'There's a bus?'

'Yeah, passes through at eight, comes back at four. How am I supposed to kill all those hours in a supermarket?'

Emily watched the girl as she returned to the counter. She poked at one protruding knitting needle, giving it a tug and then a little adjustment, frowning as she did so.

'If you're not doing anything tomorrow morning, I'd be happy to give you a lift,' Emily said. 'I have no plans.'

'Really?'

'Sure.'

For a few awkward seconds the two of them stared at each other. In normal circumstances, Emily would never have picked the girl out of a lineup of potential friends, but strange things had been happening of late.

'What's your name?' she asked, realising she had no idea, and doubting the girl would ever do so much as volunteer information.

'Veronica.'

'Well, nice to meet you. I'm Emily. I'm staying at one of the holiday lets by the church.'

'Really? Are you out of your mind?'

'I just needed a change of scenery for a while.'

'I can't believe anyone would come to this pokey little nowhere by choice. What happened? Your boyfriend dumped you?'

Emily grimaced. 'Nothing so dramatic. My grandmother died three months ago. She was my only close family member.'

'Oh. What about your parents?'

The girl's demeanour suggested Emily should expect directness. She forced another smile. 'They died when I was a baby. Car crash. I don't even remember them. My grandmother brought me up.'

'That must really suck.' Then, after an awkward moment, Veronica added, 'I'm, um, sorry for your loss.'

'It's all right. We lived together. I just can't stay there right now. Too many memories.'

'I bet.'

'What about you?'

'Huh?' Veronica shrugged and rolled her eyes. 'Oh, they're all still alive. A collective pain in the bum.'

'You said this was your mother's place?'

'Well, kind of. It's more kind of mine. My mother was going to close it, but I told her I wanted to take over. Kind of like a challenge.'

'Well, you're doing great.'

'Ha. Don't make me laugh. It's what, Wednesday? I've had less than ten customers all week so far. Three of them were Skip.'

'He must like reading.'

'He doesn't get any customers either.'

Emily remembered her grandmother, and wondered how she would have reacted. For Elaine, there was no such thing as a lack of custom. At the merest hint of a low season drop-off of trade, she would have ramped up her advertising, sent Emily out to deliver flyers around the local area, offering some sort of irresistible bargain. And once customers were in the door, she was like a cake-making spider, snaring them in her candy-stringed web. Elaine, with her endless hustle and bustle combined with a deceptively sharp wit, had specialised in providing the sort of experience that customers were keen to repeat.

'You know, if you like, I can offer you a few pointers.'

'About what?'

'I've worked in catering my whole life. My grandmother ran a café. I did all the donkey work, especially as she got older.'

Veronica shrugged. 'Okay, if you have time.'

'No problem.'

'Um, thanks.' Veronica, who had been looming over the table like a multi-coloured cloud, took a couple of forced steps backward. 'I'll leave you to eat,' she said. 'I'll be just over there.'

'I don't mind the conversation. I haven't spoken to many people since I arrived.' She thought about mentioning Nathan, but wasn't sure she could keep her feelings to herself. Despite his brusqueness, he had been alluringly attractive.

'Not many people round here.'

'There was no one in the pub earlier.'

'You went in?'

'Yeah, just for a look around. I met Skip. He seemed all right. I was going to go in the shop but it was already closed.'

Veronica said nothing. She gave an uncomfortable shift as though someone had poked her in the back, then lifted a hand and began to pick at one luminous green fingernail.

'I mean, if we go up to Tesco in the morning I can get what I need, but I was hoping to support the local community a bit while I was here. My grandmother always said that was important. If you could buy local, you should, even if it cost a little more.'

Veronica's only response was a shrug. She moved her attention on to another nail.

'Don't you get any of your supplies from there? They must sell milk and tomato sauce?'

Veronica shook her head. 'Don't go in there.'

'Why not?'

The girl grimaced, then shook her head without looking up. 'Peter might be in there,' she said.

8

PROHIBITION

A COUPLE OF PACKETS OF CRISPS SHE HAD IN HER suitcase would fill the remainder of the gap that Veronica's lovingly prepared sausage roll had failed to do, Emily was sure. As she walked back to her holiday let, she thought about the single telling phrase which had helped define the girl.

'Peter is your boyfriend?' Emily had asked.

A shrug. 'Kind of. Well, maybe. No. I don't know.'

Before Emily could clarify anything, Veronica had turned and disappeared into the kitchen. She was gone a long time, during which Emily finished the rest of the soggy, lukewarm sausage roll and drank her tea. Wondering if the girl had perhaps gone home, she got up, left a ten pound note on the counter—more than double the marked price—then called, 'I'll pop around in the morning!' before heading out into the dark.

It was only a little after seven p.m. when she got back to her holiday let. Lights were on in the pub windows on the other side of the village green, but Emily saw no one inside. It was only Wednesday, so perhaps at the weekend it would see more action. In any case, she hadn't yet spent much time getting to know the house.

In the kitchen she found a complimentary bottle of local wine in the fridge, a pleasant touch which went some way to easing the abrasiveness of Nathan's demeanour. She opened it, poured herself a glass, and retired to the small living room, of which she had only taken a brief look earlier.

Cramped but cosy, a sofa faced a log fire with an armchair to the side. A TV stood in the corner. Next to the fireplace, a fresh pile of cut logs had been stacked, along with some firelighters and a box of matches. On the mantelpiece overhead was a laminated computer printout with information on how to light a fire.

With the teahouse also having a log fire—one of Emily's winter duties had been to drive out to the firewood wholesaler once a week and stock up, if possible on cherry tree wood, as Elaine considered that to have the most comforting smell—setting and starting a fire was easy. Within ten minutes, a fire flickered in the hearth, filling the room with warmth.

She tried the sofa, finding it extremely comfortable, eventually settling into a position with her back propped up by a couple of cushions against one armrest and her legs leaning over the other. Perfect. Position established, she got up, moved a coffee table into range for her wine, before browsing the selection of a small bookcase standing in the corner. As she read over the titles, however, she wished she had picked a couple from Veronica's collection to bring with her. Among a selection of particularly nightmare-inducing horror novels were a few non-fiction books, some on true crime and others on war. She finally thought she'd hit the jackpot when she pulled out a book with a Christmas tree on the front, only to find it was a list of macabre and gothic Christmas traditions from Europe.

She gave a little shake of her head. It was almost as though the owner of the holiday let had something against people being happy. Nathan—despite the astonishing looks which still gave Emily a little tickle in the stomach when she thought of him—he had come across as moody and negative. Quite the brooding hunk. But to purposefully try to create a negative experience for one of his guests?

Emily shrugged. Perhaps a previous occupant had left the books behind.

However, the selection of DVDs wasn't much better: several bargain bin horrors and a series of documentaries on serial killers.

Luckily, Emily had brought her laptop with her, so she went and got it from her bag and set it up to roam for a Wi-Fi signal in order that she could watch something more festive online.

But … nothing. No connection. She found her phone, but she only had ten percent battery, and after a frantic search realised she had left her charger at home. Sure, it was only a half-hour drive, but she had now been drinking, albeit only a sip. Frustrated, she returned to the living room, grabbed the least horrifying of the novels and picked up her wine, which had now warmed up due to its proximity to the fire.

'Merry Christmas,' she whispered to no one, taking a sip, having a sudden moment of clarity that she was a fish out of water, had no business being here, and really shouldn't be trying to enjoy herself anyway. She was running away from her life, trying to hide her sorrows behind a pretence.

Sooner or later she would wake up, smell the coffee, and get on with her life.

But she supposed that in order for that to happen, she needed to go to bed first. The time had somehow crept on to nearly nine o'clock, but it had been a long day. She downed the last of her glass of wine, then checked the fire to make sure it would burn itself out safely.

Upstairs, she took a shower and put on her pajamas. As she went to get into bed, she paused, went over to the window and peered through a crack in the curtains at the square outside. The lights were still on in the pub. A couple of men were playing pool, but there were no other customers she could see. A couple of lights lit up the front of the church, and three streetlights cast a pretty glow over the village green.

All she'd heard since she arrived was people bemoaning the remoteness of Cottonwood, how it was a dead-end village in the middle of nowhere, but when you ignored all the criticism, it really was quite pretty. Emily could only imagine now pleasant it might be with a few benches on the village green, a couple of quaint restaurants with tables spilling out into the road. And at Christmas time, it would surely look splendid with a tall, illuminated tree in the green's centre, a few stalls selling Christmas food and treats, perhaps a small stage for some carol singers, and a line of fireworks exploding into the sky.

She sighed. It was exactly the kind of thing her grandmother would have talked about. Perhaps Emily had more of Elaine in her than she had ever realised.

Just as she was about to close the curtains and turn away, movement caught her eye. A figure had appeared from the road to the right, wearing a black jacket with a hood pulled up. Something long was held under the person's arm. From the broadness of the shoulders she surmised it was a man, even before he turned onto the green and walked up the gentle slope to the centre. There, he lifted up the object he had been holding. For a few seconds Emily was unable to see what he was doing, then he stepped away, and in the light of the streetlights she saw a signboard had been pushed into the ground.

As the man walked away, back down the road to disappear into the dark, Emily gave a surprised shake of her head. Even at this distance the words on the sign were big enough to read:

KEEP OFF THE GRASS.

9

PETER

When Emily got up the next morning and pulled open the curtains, she found a small group of people standing around in front of the new sign, arms folded, shaking their heads. Ironically, every single one of them was standing on the grass they were being warned to keep off.

Emily took a shower and changed, then went downstairs. She could vaguely remember arranging to pick Veronica up at ten, but aside from the wine she hadn't yet drunk and a tub of margarine at the back which had probably been left by previous guests, the fridge was empty and she had nothing for breakfast. Donning her jacket, she headed out.

Clear skies greeted her, bringing along with them a chilly wind rattling up from the valley. Cottonwood's orientation seemed to have left it as a bit of a wind tunnel for the surrounding hills, and by the time she had crossed the street to the shop, her hair was so messy she was holding it down with one hand while wishing she had thought to wear a hat.

The shop was uninspiringly named Cottonwood Stores. It was in an old stone building separated from the pub by a single residential property, and with all three having a similar look, Emily surmised they had probably been farm cottages or the backs of old stables facing an internal courtyard. Cottonwood had the feel of a way station. Long before the A30 had been built a few miles to the south, Cottonwood might have been a stagecoach stop for travelers heading southwest from Exeter down to Launceston and Truro. Emily wondered if that sense of transit had left an impression on the locals. Her welcome had been somewhat truncated, that was for sure.

Inside, the shop was cramped, but pleasantly stocked with everything a short-stay visitor would need, albeit at a premium compared to local supermarket prices. Taking a basket and filling it with milk, bread, cereal, a few toiletries, and some canned goods in case she needed a quick meal in a fix, she remembered her grandmother's old mantra.

'Buying local is not just buying local, Emily,' Elaine had said on more occasions that Emily could remember. 'Buying local is creating connections, building relationships, and supporting the community. Tourists come and go, but the community is your heart. Always build a good, strong heart.'

As she wandered around, adding a newspaper and a couple of out-of-date women's magazines from a rack by the door, the business mind her grandmother had installed in her over the years couldn't help but pick out issues the shop needed to address: the lack of local produce, daily offers, fresh goods, flyers for home delivery services catering for the elderly who likely made up the majority of the village's population. She was still thinking about how Elaine would have improved things when she turned to see a sullen young man watching her from behind the counter.

'All right?' he said, sounding anything but. 'Can I get you anything?'

Emily was momentarily speechless. This had to be Peter, the boy Veronica had mentioned. At a guess, he was about twenty. He looked like he wanted to be Paul Weller but with greasier hair encircling the sides of his face. A suit jacket with enough frays to suggest a charity shop purchase was open to the waist, a black and white tie loosely encircling his neck. His shirt was untucked.

'Um, I'm okay for a minute,' Emily said. 'Do you have any Marmite?'

'Over there, next to the jam.'

'Ah, I see it. Thanks.'

She could feel his eyes on her back as she retrieved a jar and put it into her basket. He looked quickly away as she turned around. She carried the basket over to the counter and set it down. As he began to ring up the items she noticed the way he kept glancing up at her and decided to put him out of his misery.

'No, I'm not from round here,' she said.

His head snapped up. His eyes widened, then he looked away. Red plumed in his cheeks. 'I didn't—'

'I thought you might have wondered. I'm guessing you don't get a lot of through-trade.'

'The odd person stops by for a newspaper but never for a weekly shop,' he said.

Emily hadn't considered the nine items in her basket a weekly shop, but supposed Cottonwood Stores was as affected by the rise in internet shopping and home delivery as every other rural community. She had probably doubled his weekly profits.

'I'm staying over at one of the holiday lets,' she said. 'I like to shop local when I can.'

'It's much appreciated. Why on earth would you want to stay here? And at one of them….'

This last was said as an aside as his eyes dropped, his thoughts trailing off, but Emily picked up enough of the tone. Birchtide was a little bigger than Cottonwood, but even so, it had its share of local politics. Villagers had almost gone to war over such minor things as speed bumps, public-rights-of-way, and the hygiene—or not, depending on the person—of dog walkers. Resentments and feuds could often run generations deep.

'I needed a break,' Emily said. 'Family stuff. I was looking for somewhere quiet to relax.'

'Well, you won't find much quieter.'

'Are you local?'

'Unfortunately so. I'm home from university for the holidays. I wanted to stay up in Manchester, but you know, my mum would get upset.'

Emily smiled. 'You must be Peter.'

'Uh, yeah. How'd you know?'

Wary of undercurrents of which she might not be aware, Emily chose her words carefully. 'I met someone who mentioned you, that's all. Her name was Veronica. Over at the café?'

Peter's cheeks flared again. Despite an odd choice of clothing which suggested a certain level of confidence, at the mention of Veronica he became as awkward as a fourteen-year-old asked for a first dance.

'Oh, her. Yeah, I know her.'

Emily decided not to force it. 'I was just asking where I might pick up a few things, and she said you could help.'

'Well, great. Yeah, there's not much here, but it'll, you know, keep you alive.'

'Thanks.' Emily took the plastic bag Peter had filled with her groceries and decided to put him out of his misery. 'Anyway, thanks, and nice to meet you. I'll see you around.'

'Sure.'

Outside, the wind had eased and the air had taken on a welcome warmth. The sun hung low above the buildings to the east. Emily gave it a quick glance before heading back across the square to her holiday let. In the kitchen, she made herself coffee, cereal, and toast with Marmite. Her phone's battery was completely dead, but she found an old transistor radio in a cupboard behind the kitchen door, and when plugged in she was able to tune it to Radio 2, which was playing a selection of Christmas songs.

With the sun streaming in the kitchen window and Frank Sinatra crooning on the radio, she felt more positive than she had in weeks. Perhaps, in this lonely little place, she could make a pleasant Christmas for herself.

Something wasn't quite right about the village, though. There had been something about the shop that had been odd, but at the time she had been unable to put her finger on quite what it was. Now, after some time of reflection, it was obvious.

It was Thursday, December the twelfth. Christmas was barely two weeks away. Yet, neither inside nor outside the shop, nor on any other building, for that matter, Emily hadn't seen a single Christmas decoration.

10

SHOPPING

Tree & Decorations. Turkey. Stuffing Mix. Phone charger.

Emily jotted down what she needed on a pad of paper next to a phone in the hall. Then, next to each item, she put an asterisk if she could buy it anywhere other than a major supermarket.

Might as well practice what she preached.

At nine-thirty she packed her bag and headed out to her car. She was just searching for her keys when a polite voice with a sing-song quality came from behind her.

'Good morning.'

She turned to find two young boys, no older than eleven or twelve, standing behind her. One was carrying a frisbee. The one who had spoken smiled and pointed at the village green.

'There's a sign,' he said. 'Does that mean we can't play on there?' The other boy cocked his head as though also anticipating the answer.

Emily grimaced. 'Boys, I'm afraid I'm not local. I'd say that you should do as the sign says. Isn't there somewhere else you can play?'

Both heads visibly sagged. The boy who had spoken sighed. The other turned to him and said, 'Can't we play in one of your dad's fields?'

'Let's go and ask.'

With a brief goodbye to Emily, they headed off, up the left-hand fork past the pub and shop. Emily watched them go, their shoulders slumped, talking quietly as they walked. She gave a brief shake of her head, understanding the point of the sign now. Today was the first day of the school Christmas holidays. It was quite clear that Cottonwood had a Scrooge hiding somewhere behind one of its tall hedgerows.

With another bemused shake of her head, she climbed into her car and went to fetch Veronica.

∾

The girl hadn't dressed down. If anything, she had spent the evening preening herself, adding extra layers of intrigue and colour. A couple of new lines of sky blue had appeared in hair hanging down the sides of her face, while her nails were freshly painted. She wore a t-shirt with the slogan *Art is Life* on the front, with what Emily could only describe as a technicolour jacket over the top. It looked like someone had sewn together several multi-coloured toilet mats.

'Thanks,' Veronica said, setting into place like a peacock preparing to roost. 'Are you getting on okay?'

Emily shrugged. 'I suppose. I feel a bit isolated.'

With a smile she hoped might make her seem young and hip, she said, 'I forgot my phone charger.'

'Nightmare,' Veronica said, deadpan. 'You can't get much signal anyway. They might as well put a fence up and forget about us.'

'Who's they?'

'The outside world.'

'You don't seem to like it here too much.'

'Yeah, I do,' Veronica said, in complete contrast to her attitude. 'I love it. Got my business, my friends, everything really.'

'It must be nice,' Emily said, trying not to sound sarcastic. 'It feels like a very close-knit community.'

Veronica just shrugged.

They drove on for a while in silence. Veronica stared straight ahead, as though to turn her head might upset the delicate balance of her appearance.

'I thought we could hit up the supermarket first,' Emily said. 'Just to get the essentials. Then we could go round a couple of farm shops.'

'Sure.'

'Is there anywhere in particular you'd like to go?'

'Nope.'

Emily waited a few seconds for any elaboration before playing her trump card. 'I, um, met Peter,' she said.

Veronica's head snapped around. 'Did he mention me?'

'No, I'm afraid not. I didn't really talk to him. He seems nice, though.'

Veronica turned to stare out of the front again, but her head was swaying gently from side to side.

Emily wondered if she could describe the motion as a visual representation of swooning.

'Did you grow up together?'

'Yeah.'

'He looked about your age.'

A shrug. 'Six months older. Ruined everything.'

Emily wasn't sure how to react. 'Ah, that's not much really, is it?'

Veronica's head snapped around again. Emily was shocked to see her eyes glistening. As the girl spoke, a single tear dribbled down through the mascara coating her cheek.

'Six months put him a year ahead at school. Didn't want to hang out with me no more.'

∽

They picked up what they needed from the supermarket and loaded it into the back of Emily's car. Enough condiments to see Veronica's café through to the New Year, plus a few luxury items Emily said would add an extra touch. Away from the awkward issues of social interaction and back to professing Elaine's business wisdom, Emily was in her element.

'For a start, your menus need to go,' she said. 'You've got way too much crossed off. If you can't sell it, don't have it on there. Tell the customer what you do have, not what you don't.'

'I see.'

'Use a specials board for anything new or different. Specials are important, too. While you'll get a certain percentage of your clientele who'll always order the same thing, there's another subset always looking for something new.'

'Got it.'

'And get something on there for the special dietary groups. The vegetarians, vegans, the gluten-free. They're expanding their market share all the time, but more importantly, if you get big groups, chances are there'll be one person with a special dietary requirement. If you can't satisfy it, you could lose five or six other customers at the same time.'

Veronica had pulled out a phone and appeared to be typing notes. 'Did you go to business school?'

Emily smiled. 'I did a couple of courses, but better than that, I lived with a good coach.'

'Your grandmother?'

'Yeah. She built up her business from nothing, practically single-handed. By the time she died, it was the biggest private business in our village.' *And it's been sat empty ever since*, a little voice whispered. 'Ah, here we are,' Emily said louder than was necessary, drowning it out.

'Where?'

Emily pointed up at the sign outside the industrial holding. 'Royston Lumber Yard,' she said. 'Also known at this time of year as a Christmas tree wholesaler.'

'But I don't have a Christmas tree.'

'That's why we're here.'

'But—'

'No buts.' Emily pulled into a car parking space and killed the engine. Before Veronica could say anything else, she jumped out of the car and headed for the wholesaler's entrance. Behind her, she heard a car door open and close, then a low sigh as Veronica trailed after her like a sullen child.

The lumber yard's manager was a monster of a man who looked like he uprooted the trees himself.

'Barney!' Emily greeted her old friend warmly as Bernard Collins came out of a porta-cabin office to greet her. Huge hands made bigger by workman's gloves swallowed hers like a pelican gobbling down a fish.

'Young Miss Wilson,' Barney said, reaching up to pick a bit of sawdust out of his thick, wiry beard. 'I was so sorry to hear about Elaine's passing. I do hope you're keeping okay.'

Emily forced a smile. 'I'm getting there,' she said.

'To what do I owe this visit?'

Barney and his crew had built the wooden terrace at the back of Elaine's teahouse, and came by once every couple of years to make sure it was holding up. In addition, Elaine had bought her Christmas trees here for as long as Emily could remember.

'I'm after a couple of trees,' she said.

'For the teahouse? I have just—'

Emily put up a hand. 'I'm downscaling a little this year. Taking a holiday. I'm not ready to reopen just yet.' *I might never be ready.* 'I'm, um, helping a friend. This is Veronica.' She stepped back, waving the younger girl forward. Veronica just nodded.

'All right?' she said.

'She has a small café and book exchange in Cottonwood,' Emily said, sensing Veronica wasn't about to make her own case. 'Have you got many trees left?'

'Come and take a look.'

Veronica, appearing more disinterested the longer the visit went on, trailed Emily as Barney led them deep into the lumber yard. In a shed at the back they found dozens of cut pine trees, tied up in netting. They ran from less than a metre tall to some over five metres.

'What size should we go for?' Emily asked the girl.

Veronica just shrugged. 'Dunno.'

'How big's your room?' Barney asked.

'Not so big.'

'Well, how about a one-fifty? They spring outwards and you can blag a bit of extra height by putting it on a little table.'

'Sure,' Veronica said.

'Can you make it two?' Emily asked. 'I want one for where I'm staying.' Out of the corner of her eye she caught a sharp glance from Veronica, but she ignored it.

'Sure. I'll get one of the lads to lash them to your roof rack. On the account?'

Emily, who hadn't realised she still had an account open with Royston's, just nodded. 'Sure.'

Veronica, for her part, showed no interest in being involved in any of the discussions. She stayed out in the yard, fiddling with her nails or occasionally withdrawing a smartphone for a quick email check, while Emily had a brief conversation with Barney inside the porta-cabin office.

'Wherever did you find her?' Barney asked.

'In the village where I'm staying. Cottonwood. She seemed interested in a few pointers to smarten up her business, but now I'm not so sure.'

Barney laughed. 'She's barely out of her teens. She probably has issues.'

Emily laughed and agreed, but she wasn't so sure. Labelling Veronica as anything less than complex would be a mistake.

By the time Barney led her back out to her car, the two trees had been strapped on to her roof rack. Emily waved goodbye to Barney, then climbed into the car. Veronica climbed in beside her, staring straight ahead. Emily wondered if she ought to say something, but as they pulled out of the lumber yard and back on to the road, Veronica suddenly twisted in the seat.

'You'll get told off, you know.'

'What for?'

'That tree. I wanted to tell you, but I didn't know how to bring it up. We're not allowed Christmas decorations in Cottonwood. Nothing with electric lights at any rate.'

'What are you talking about?'

'It's the rule,' Veronica said.

'Whose rule?'

'The suits. Cottonwood Parish Council. No electric decorations of any kind, and if you can't have a few lights, not a lot of point having a tree, is there?'

11

WINSTON

'Okay, so run that by me again, because I'm having a bit of trouble believing it all.'

Veronica, sitting across the table with a cup of coffee held in two hands, gave a shrug. 'The parish council voted to make Cottonwood part of a Devonshire eco-zone. A new government initiative, apparently. Every property is on a meter, as is the village as a whole. We have to stick to a certain level of electrical output, otherwise it cuts off.'

'That sounds ridiculous. You voted for this?'

Veronica shook her head. 'No. The parish council did. Mum just got a letter through the door.'

'And people just put up with it?'

Veronica shrugged. 'Yeah. I think a few got angry at first, but whatever.'

'So what happened?'

'This time of year we need heating, so you have to be frugal elsewhere. The parish council put an unofficial ban on Christmas tree lights.'

Emily coughed. 'Did I drive ten miles south and arrive in Dickensian England?'

'What?'

'It's just so … bizarre. When was this?'

Veronica frowned. 'Uh … would be two years ago. Christmas before last.'

'So you've had two Christmases without any lights?'

'Year before a few people protested, but last year, yeah. No one wanted to stand out, so no one bothered.'

Emily shook her head. 'You just ignored Christmas?'

Veronica shrugged again. 'Drank some wine, watched the TV.'

Mystified at such bizarre behaviour, at least it explained the letter still tucked inside her jacket pocket. Written two years ago, perhaps after the first crackdown on any fairy lights. And after last year, when no answer came, perhaps the writer had now given up.

They made small talk for a while before Emily excused herself. She glanced down at the Christmas tree propped up next to the door, wondering if she ought to just take it back. 'What should I do with this?' she asked.

'Dunno. I might put a bit of tinsel on it, I suppose. Put it out in the back room. If it gets seen, see, they might come round and complain, accuse me of hiding lights on it somewhere.'

'Has this ever happened?'

'Not yet, but you don't want it to, do you?'

For Emily, Cottonwood and its irregularities had proven something of a distraction, but now she felt a sudden urge to cry. Christmas had been when her grandmother truly came alive, transforming the teahouse into a glowing, vibrating heaven of Christmas cheer and excitement. The teahouse had been packed nearly every day from the beginning of December right through New Year, Elaine's endless charm welcoming people and sending them on their way with a glowing smile and raucous laughter.

'I'll see you later,' she said, needing to get out of the café as quickly as she could. Tears filled her eyes as she walked back to her holiday let, eyes down. It had begun to drizzle, and she was happy to get inside and lock the door behind her, shutting Cottonwood outside.

Her suitcase, emptied of its belongings, stood at the bottom of the stairs where she had left it. It wouldn't take much to pack and throw it back in the car. She would lose what she had paid on the let, but money wasn't an issue.

Then she thought of the closed teahouse and all the nostalgia she would have to face. She couldn't go back, not yet. And the only alternative was to take Karen up on her offer and put up with David's perfect, saccharine-drenched family over the Christmas period.

She went into the living room and slumped down on the sofa in front of the fire. No, she couldn't leave just yet. What would Elaine have done? Her grandmother certainly wouldn't have walked away.

No, she had come here to relax and escape from

her memories for a while. She was getting too invested in the problems of other people. What had she been expecting? A great Christmas carnival in the village square?

She listed on her fingers her reasons to stay. Rest. Relaxation. Finding the writer of the letter. The … handsome landlord.

She smiled. Things could be worse.

As she let her thoughts return to him, however, she wondered if perhaps he knew about the supposed ban on Christmas decorations. Perhaps that was why he had planned to close his holiday lets over Christmas; to save someone the disappointment. As Veronica said, however, it was only a ban on electric lights; no one was stopping her putting up the tree and wrapping some tinsel around it.

She checked her watch. She had spent most of the day with Veronica and it was nearly three o'clock. Sunset would come around four, with it being fully dark by half past. In the hallway, she pulled on her shoes and jacket and headed out for a walk around the village.

First she turned right out of her front door and headed up the fork to the right of the church. The houses quickly thinned out, gaining size and value the farther she went from the village square. Past a couple of semis which opened out onto the road were larger houses with front gardens, followed by even bigger residences with driveways leading through trees to houses barely visible. She caught the glimpse of one large old house, guessing it had once been the home of a local landowner. Steeped in history, she had already guessed her own house might have once housed farm workers, perhaps several at a time, and here, at the end of the village, were the residences of the people who might once have employed them.

Beyond the largest of the houses, the road narrowed and snaked away into rolling farmland, a few neighbouring villages visible across the hills. The sun was almost set, however, so Emily turned back, taking a narrow intersecting lane that appeared to lead behind the church.

She hadn't brought a torch but figured if it took an unexpected turn and started leading away from Cottonwood, she could easily retrace her steps, but it quickly dipped into a valley she hadn't even known was there, trees rising around her to loom over the road, cutting off most of the lingering light.

By the time she had reached a ford over a gentle stream at the bottom of the valley, Emily had committed to taking on the circuit. Feeling a little nervous as she walked in near darkness, she kept one eye on the break in the trees overhead even as the hedgerows became amorphous lumps to either side. She was climbing out of the valley now, passing on the way a couple of driveways that led to houses identified only by distant lights through the trees. The rise of the hill should be right in front of her, but she continued to climb, unable to see anything now, her panic slowly rising. Birchtide, while not much bigger than Cottonwood, was entirely flat, its only wooded areas set a long way back from the roads and accessible only along footpaths. As the road began to flatten out and then, to Emily's horror, dip back into the valley, she felt her heart starting to race.

Wait it out, wait it out. This is England, not some wilderness.

Her self-assurances meant nothing as she felt the trees, so close to parting, now close in again. She was walking almost blind, her rising terror urging her to get a move on, to get out of these woods as soon as possible.

She broke into a jog, running blindly, aware that it was a stupid idea but unable to help herself. The road felt damp and crumbly under her feet, and she began to worry that she had taken some dead end, that the road would come out at an abandoned quarry she would stumble into in the dark. Even the houses she had passed felt miles behind, and she started to wonder if climbing the hedge and hoping there was an open field on the other side might not be a good idea.

Then, as quickly as she had been running, she felt her feet slip, one caught on a pothole or loose piece of tarmac. She stumbled forward, her knees hitting the ground, a cry of pain escaping her lips before she could help herself.

A dog barked, far closer than she would have liked.

'Winston, wait a minute!'

The man's voice came from somewhere ahead, but Emily didn't have much time to register it because something with scratching paws and a slobbering mouth was rushing toward her. Was this a hound, something with sharp teeth ready to rip out her throat? It sounded enormous, huge feet bounding over the loose dirt on the road. She heard a whine so close it was right in her ear, and she closed her eyes, waiting for the teeth.

'No, please!'

A huge wet lump slid its way up the side of her face. Something that felt and smelled like a bundle of old rugs pressed against her. She opened her eyes as a light clicked on, illuminating the ground at her feet and a great grey-white shape which was revolving in circles. A hand reached down for a collar and the revolutions stopped. A great lolling tongue flopped out below cords of thick hair which almost covered a pair of beady black eyes.

'I'm so sorry about that,' came the man's voice again. 'Winston does tend to get excited when he meets new people. I hope he didn't slime you too bad.'

Emily, relieved just to meet someone on this dark and terrifying road, shook her head. 'It'll wash off,' she said.

12

ROWE FARM

Barely a hundred metres farther on, the road had taken a sharp left turn back up the hill, emerged out of the trees and passed the entrance to Alan Rowe's farm. Alan, the man in charge of both the torch and the excitable Old English Sheepdog called Winston, led her down the lane toward a large farmhouse standing at the end.

'We'll clean up your cuts, get you a cup of tea, and then I'll drop you back to the square,' he said. 'It's only a mile, but you're clearly not from round here and it can be a bit terrifying in the dark. It gets proper dark round here, as they say. You're from Exeter or farther afield?'

Emily felt sheepish as she answered, 'Birchtide.'

'Really? That's just up the road.'

'I fancied a change of scenery.'

'Not much of one, but I suppose each to their own. Right, here we are.'

They had come to a stop outside the farmhouse,

which now towered above them. Alan led Emily into an open porch while Winston, now back on his lead, sniffed and whined with nervous excitement.

The front door was an old hardwood which creaked as Alan pushed it open. From inside came the smell of fresh bread, and Emily blinked in the bright lights of a hallway that reminded her of a log cabin with its wood-finished walls and arches leading off into several rooms.

'John, Lily! Put the kettle on, won't you? We have a guest.'

Alan kicked off his boots, then attempted to wipe Winston with a towel. The dog, panting with delight, shook it off, slipped his lead, and raced inside. Alan shouted at the kids to keep the dog off the sofa, then turned and rolled his eyes at Emily as though he expected his request to be ignored.

Getting a look at him for the first time, Emily estimated Alan was in his mid-thirties, although his thick beard made labelling him difficult. He was broad-shouldered, with a mop of hazelnut brown hair held down by a baseball cap. He had a kind smile and warm eyes which felt fitting to his house.

'Welcome to Rowe Farm,' he said, waving her inside. 'Let's get you fixed up.'

He led her through into a kitchen as lovingly created as the hall. Shining marble work surfaces contrasted the colours of the wood paneling. It felt like a cottage but modern at the same time, the kind of kitchen one might find in a lifestyle magazine about sustainable modern living.

'John, have you put the kettle on yet? Kids, this is Emily. I found her wandering about in the dark.'

The two children appeared out of a side door to stand in front of her. The girl was around nine or ten, with hair tied back in a ponytail and furtive, searching eyes. The boy, a smaller version of his dad but without the beard, looked familiar. As his eyes widened in recognition, Emily remembered.

'You're the lady I met this morning,' he said, getting in before Emily could say something herself. 'Up at the green. Are you staying around here?'

'Yes, up in the village.'

'What were you doing wandering around in the dark?'

'I went for a walk around the village but I got lost.'

Alan put a hand on the boy's shoulder. 'John, remember your manners. Emily's had a fall, so let's show her some Rowe hospitality, shall we?'

'Sorry, Dad. I'll make the tea.'

'Thanks, lad.'

As John ran off, Alan turned to the girl. 'My daughter, Lilian. We call her Lily. The unstoppable force of nature that is my son is John, in case you didn't catch it.'

'My name's Emily,' Emily said. 'Your father was kind enough to help me after I got lost.' She grinned as Winston, more of a carpet on legs than a dog, came racing in from a side entrance, gave her a brief acknowledgement and then put his front paws on Lily's chest as the girl staggered backward. 'And I met the dog, too.'

'He's friendly,' Lily said. 'He gets hair everywhere, though.'

'Down!' Alan said, with the kind of exasperated tone that suggested he expected to be ignored. The dog did a circle around Lily's feet, then ran off into another room.

The social whirlwind of the Rowe household exhausted Emily so much that she was glad to be offered a chair at a dining room table. She pulled up her jeans to reveal a gash on her right knee. Alan took some Dettox and a box of plasters out of a cupboard while the kids hovered behind him.

'I'll let you patch yourself up,' he said, handing Emily the disinfectant. 'Looks rough, but it's just a scratch. Be fixed in no time.'

'Thanks.'

'You should be careful out there, though. Especially when you don't know the roads. The hedges on the forest side have collapsed in a few places.'

'I was trying to loop back to the village. The road looked like it would swing back around to the church.'

'Oh, it does, it just takes its sweet time about it. That's the thing with these country roads. They can go on for miles.'

A few minutes later, patched up, and with a warm cup of tea in her hands, Emily felt much better. Relaxing in the Rowes' large dining-living room, she felt as comfortable as at any time since her arrival.

'Would you like to stay for dinner?' Alan asked. 'It's only bread, soup, and a few boiled vegetables. I'm afraid I'm not much of a cook.'

'And we have treacle tart!' Lily called from her place on the sofa, where she and John were watching children's TV.

'Supermarket-bought,' Alan said. 'Cooking desserts is a bit beyond me.'

'I could teach you how to make one sometime if you like,' Emily said, the words bouncing off her tongue before she realised they were there. 'It's not that difficult. My grandmother ran a teahouse. All the cakes were home-cooked. She was a master at treacle tart.'

'Well, thanks. I suppose we'll need to get some stuff cooked for Christmas. Are you staying in Cottonwood over the holiday period?'

'I had planned to.'

Alan briefly lifted an eyebrow, followed by a slight shake of his head. 'I suppose if you were looking for quiet, you couldn't find anywhere much quieter.' He looked about to say something else, but then stood up. 'I'll get something on for dinner. You'll stay, won't you? I mean, I'm not the best cook in the world, but I'm probably not the worst.'

Faced with the alternative, a microwave meal in her lonely holiday let, Emily nodded. 'I'd love to.'

'Great.'

'Emily, will you play in my room until dinner's ready?' Lily suddenly called, jumping up and leaning over the back of the sofa. 'I'll show you my stuff.'

'Um, sure.'

The girl, already taking yes for an answer, hurried over, took Emily's hand and led her upstairs to a door with a little sign on it announcing *Lily's Room*. Inside, it was a treasure trove of girls' toys, all drenched in a nauseating pink so bright Emily was sure she could taste candy floss in the air.

'You be Barbie, I'll be Ken,' Lily announced, thrusting a doll dressed in a ballroom gown into Emily's hand.

'How pretty. Are they going dancing?'

Lily shook her head. 'No, no. To the zoo.'

'Oh.'

'The hippo is sick,' she said, holding up a plastic animal. 'He needs to go to the doctor. Barbie's the doctor and Ken's the paramedic.'

'Right.'

Emily smiled and played along as Lily explained an increasingly fantastical scenario, doing what she was told and adding the odd embellishment where she felt it necessary. None of her close friends had children, and her own childhood was so long ago that if she had once played like this, she no longer remembered. It felt nice, casual, but even so, there was something missing. It took Emily a moment to figure it out.

'Christmas is coming soon,' she said, wanting to skirt around the question to put Lily at ease. 'Have you asked Father Christmas for anything?'

Lily shrugged. 'One or two things.'

'Do you think you'll get them?'

Another shrug. 'I might. I've been a good girl this year.'

'I, um, noticed you didn't have a Christmas tree up yet.'

Lily shook her head. 'No, not yet.'

'When will you put it up?'

'Next week maybe. We only have a small one.'

'Is there any reason why you put it up so late?'

Lily looked up, fixing Emily with a stare. 'Dad says he doesn't want to upset anyone.'

'Who would he upset?'

Lily sighed. 'The man who doesn't like Christmas trees.'

'And who's that?'

'I don't know his name, but he lives in a big house.'

'Where?'

'In Cottonwood. The biggest house.'

Emily smiled. 'Maybe I'll have a word with him, and tell him to stop being so silly,' she said, wondering if it wouldn't be a bad idea at all. Putting a restriction on celebrating Christmas seemed so ridiculous.

'Would you?'

'Sure.'

'Great.'

The girl looked about to say something more, but from downstairs Alan's voice came faintly through the floor, calling them down for dinner.

'Did you have to play animal rescue?' Alan said, giving Lily a sideways glance as they took their places around the table. 'I'm hoping Lily'll want to be a vet when she grows up.'

'I enjoyed it,' Emily said. 'I haven't played like that in … well, since I was a child.'

'Will you come over again?' Lily asked.

'If I'm invited.'

'Shut up,' John said, kicking her chair. 'Stop trying to change this around.'

'Leave your sister alone,' Alan said, taking his seat. 'Remember, we have a guest.'

'It's all right,' Emily said.

Alan smiled. 'They just get excited having a visitor. It doesn't happen often.'

The dinner was basic but filling and wholesome, with no signs of plastic or packaging until the treacle tart appeared at the end. Elaine would have approved. As Emily declined a second piece, she leaned back in her chair, far fuller than she had expected.

'How was it?' Alan asked.

'Excellent. Best meal I've had in ages.'

'Ah, you're just being kind.'

'You haven't seen what I've been eating.'

'What have you been eating, Emily?' Lily blurted, but before Emily could answer, she added, 'Why did you come to Cottonwood?'

Unsure how much the children could understand, she said, 'Well, I needed a break from things. My grandmother died a few months ago, and it's been a struggle.'

The atmosphere at the table immediately changed. John's smile vanished, and Alan looked as though he would rather be in the kitchen, washing up. Lily, however, leaned closer, the questions bubbling on her lips.

'How old was she?'

'Um, eighty-seven.'

'That's pretty old, isn't it?'

'Yes, but she was more like a mother to me.'

'Where's your mother?'

'Ah … she died when I was very young. I don't even remember her.'

'My mother's dead too. I remember her a little. She's over there on the shelf.'

As the girl pointed at a photograph sitting on a shelf near the TV, John jumped up and ran out of the room.

'Lily, can you hold the questions, please,' Alan said.

'But Dad—'

'Enough. We don't need to talk about this right now.'

Emily slowly stood up. 'Look, I think I should go. I'm sure I'll be okay, but if you could lend me a torch—'

'Nonsense,' Alan said. 'I'll give you a lift back in the car. It's not far. I'm sorry about this.'

'It's fine.'

'I'll just get my keys.'

Alan went out into the hall. Emily heard quiet voices, before Alan reappeared with John trailing behind him. The boy wiped his nose on his sleeve and refused to meet Emily's eyes.

'Shoes on, Lily,' Alan said. 'I'm not leaving you behind.'

'Is Winston coming?'

'No. Someone has to look after the house.'

Eventually, Alan managed to herd the children to the doorway and get their shoes on. Emily, worried that she had inadvertently created tension between them, hung back, waiting until Alan and the children were ready. Then together, they went outside.

Alan led them to a Land Rover parked in a shed to the left. The kids bundled into the back while Emily got up into the front. In a vehicle, the distance back to the square seemed nothing at all, and within a couple of minutes Alan was pulling up outside the village green.

'There's the sign, Dad,' John said, pointing at the KEEP OFF THE GRASS sign poking up in the middle of the grassy area.

'Rules are rules, John,' Alan said, but under his breath added, 'He'll ruin this place.' Emily didn't like to ask who Alan was referring to, so she just thanked him for the ride and climbed out.

'Take care,' Alan said, as the kids chorused in with goodbyes, Lily's a little more enthusiastic than John's.

Emily watched the Land Rover drive off. Despite the awkwardness, the sulks, and the relentless noise, she found she missed them already.

With a sigh, she headed for her holiday let.

13
CLOSURES

In the morning, Emily figured to hell with the parish council's rules and set up her tree. The only downside was that after Veronica's revelation, they hadn't bothered to buy any decorations. She did a search of the holiday let's cupboards but found nothing. After a couple of days in Cottonwood, she was feeling a little claustrophobic, plus she needed to check the teahouse's post, so she headed back to Birchtide. There, in the garage at the back, she found Elaine's treasure trove of Christmas decorations, several boxes of fairy lights, tree ornaments, garden displays, some singing toys and even a couple of Father Christmas costumes. Elaine had always dressed up at Christmas, taking on the role of Father Christmas, with Emily alternating between an elf and a fairy, depending on her mood. One of Elaine's joys had been to burst into random song, encouraging the customers to sing along, so in the evenings they had practiced to the point where there wasn't a Christmas song even vaguely famous for which Emily didn't recall the words.

She only just managed to get all the boxes of decorations into the car. Afterward, she retrieved the post, before pausing for a moment in the empty teahouse's dining room, feeling both a wave of nostalgia and regret, plus a hint of guilt that by taking the decorations she was beginning the gutting process in her grandmother's passing, and that piece by piece the teahouse and her memories would fade until eventually nothing was left. With a sigh, she went back to the car, sitting in it for a long time before turning on the engine.

Just as she was about to pull away, her phone buzzed. Karen. Emily put the handbrake back on while she answered.

'Hi, how are you doing?' came Karen's cheerful voice. 'Are you still in Cottonwood? Did you find out who wrote that letter yet?'

'Well, yes and no. I'm there, but I'm not currently there are the moment, if that makes sense. And no, not yet. Although I've met a few people, so I might have without knowing it.'

Relieved to be talking to someone who understood her, she went over what had happened in Cottonwood over the last couple of days.

'What a strange place,' Karen said at last. 'Who'd ever think to ban the use of fairy lights? I mean, haven't they heard of solar power? Most of the outdoor ones you get these days have a little solar panel you plug into the ground somewhere. Are you going to upset the status quo and cause a scandal?'

Emily grinned. 'I most certainly am.'

'Well, when you rile them up and get a big Christmas carnival started, give me a shout and I'll get David's clan to drive over en masse. Always nice to get out of the house for a while. David's father thinks he's Chevy Chase in *National Lampoon*, and there's only so much of that cheesiness I can handle. Plus, the boys, there being seven of them, are constantly breaking into that irritating dwarf song from *Snow White*. So have you seen the landlord again?'

'Not since I arrived.'

'Can't you pretend the hot water's not working or something and get him around to warm you up?'

'Karen!'

'Well, it must be dark and lonely over there if you're not allowed a Christmas tree. You've got to spend your time doing something.'

'I was planning to read a few books.'

'Oh, how exciting. Well, I've got to go. The future M-I-L is back from Waitrose so I'd better go and help her unload.'

'Sure. Speak to you soon.'

As she hung off, all the excitement Karen had pulled bubbling to the surface began to subside. Emily looked over her shoulder at the mounds of Christmas decorations piled into the back of her car. What if no one in Cottonwood wanted her intrusion? What if they were happy with their dark, windy, tree-less Christmas?

As she turned back to start the engine, she felt the press of the letter, still in the pocket inside her jacket.

Despite the impression she had got, not everyone

was happy about it, and if one person was motivated enough to write a letter about it to a tree in Germany, it was safe to assume that person wasn't alone.

∼

Cottonwood was as she had left it; quiet, gloomy and, well, more quiet. A couple of cars were parked outside the church, but there was no sign of their owners. Emily parked in her space, unlocked the holiday let's front door, and began carrying her boxes of ornaments into the house.

She had just done the third box and was coming back for the fourth when she noticed Peter from the shop standing beside her car.

'Would you like some help?' he asked her. 'I saw you through the window and, well, we're not busy.'

'Okay, thanks. If you could just take that box and bring it into the house over there. They're heavier than they look, and I'm not in the best of shape.'

Like an obedient dog, Peter did as he was told, trailing after Emily with a box of Christmas decorations in his arms. He carried it through into the kitchen and put it down on the table where Emily instructed.

They returned to the car for one final load. As Peter put it down on the floor in front of the larder, he turned to Emily and asked, 'What's all this stuff for?'

Emily smiled. 'I'm going to be staying over Christmas, so I want this place to look a bit merrier.'

'But there's enough stuff here for an entire street.'

With a nod, Emily said, 'Well, that's kind of the

plan. I thought I'd ask around, see if it was okay to put some lights up around the churchyard or on the village green.'

Peter winced as though someone had punched him in the stomach. 'You won't be allowed,' he said.

'Why not?'

'Because it's the village rules.'

'It's a stupid rule.'

Peter shrugged. 'I know that, and you know that, but I didn't decide it.'

'Who did?'

'Trower. Chairman of Cottonwood Parish Council. Him and his city mates. They applied to the government to get Cottonwood allocated as some kind of eco-village. We have to follow certain rules or we'll lose our status.'

'Like not putting up Christmas trees?'

'Saving electricity.'

'Solar-powered fairy lights?'

'Light pollution. Cottonwood is an environmental black spot.'

Emily rolled her eyes. 'I've noticed.'

'As in, it's considered a place with clean visibility. You can see more stars here than you can in other places.' He sighed. 'Well, you would if it wasn't for all the other villages and their lights which aren't part of the same system.'

'So it's a waste of time?'

'Yeah, pretty much.'

'Yet you all stick to it?'

Peter shrugged. 'Not worth the hassle of standing up against it, really. A few people tried two years ago, the first Christmas it came in, and it didn't work out too well. There used to be another pub at the other end of the village. It's closed now.'

'These people got a pub closed down for using fairy lights?'

'Kind of, yeah. Slammed it online so bad people stopped going. In a place like this your profit is minimal at the best of times. A few hard weeks and you're done.' Peter shrugged. 'You won't say anything to anyone about what I've said, will you? I mean, I don't know who you've been talking to, but some people are on Trower's side, and others not. You don't want to go around spreading rumours. It doesn't matter much to me because as soon as I graduate I'm out of here and I'm not coming back. Mum still runs the shop, though, and business hasn't been good for years.' He lowered his head. 'I probably shouldn't have said anything. I'd better go.'

Without another word, he went out, leaving Emily standing bemused in her kitchen among a jumble of boxes.

'What's going on with this place?' she muttered, giving a little shake of her head.

14

REVELATION

She started with the garden first, stringing the lights up along the fences and around the edges of a pretty pond in the bottom corner. She adorned a line of trees then set up a couple of illuminated Father Christmas figures, one riding a sleigh across the lawn, the other climbing the wall up to the rear kitchen window. At lunchtime she ate a sandwich, sitting at the kitchen table and gazing out at her handiwork, feeling a little nervous at the lights coming on tonight after the solar batteries had charged up. The lets on either side were empty, however, and there were no houses visible across the valley from the patio outside the back door. She knew that some people might consider it tacky, but the idea of being asked to switch it all off at Christmas time—especially when all the lights ran on solar power—seemed ridiculous.

Elaine had loved Christmas so much Emily could almost believe that she had died and been reincarnated as one of Father Christmas's fairies.

From the beginning of December right through until January 6th the teahouse had glowed with fairy lights. Ever creative, each year Elaine had unveiled some new style of decoration or form of illumination which she had either bought off an obscure website or made herself. Emily's favourite had been the four-foot-tall origami snowman made out of hundreds of old Christmas cards. Keeping it secret even from Emily, Elaine had spent a week in early December hiding away in a back room every evening, until the official unveiling at her big Christmas welcome party, always held on the second-to-last Saturday before Christmas, when all cakes and drinks were reduced to half price but entry required a secret Santa gift up to a cost of ten pounds to be donated at the door. Rather than giving them back to the customers, however, Elaine and Emily would drive around local kids' homes and care homes and redistribute them, along with a slice of some kind of delicious cake or pie.

Those days had been a laugh riot, driving around the local villages with a car loaded full of cakes and presents, singing Christmas songs so loud that pedestrians they passed would jump away from the road in fright.

Emily wiped away a tear. 'Miss you,' she said, sniffing as she peered out at the garden with its display of silent lights.

Next, she went into the living room and set up the tree in a corner near the window, adorning it with decorations and wrapping it with tinsel and fairy lights. She felt almost criminal as she switched off the room light and then plugged her lights into a socket in the corner. The tree lit up in an instant, filling the room with a warm glow. Emily couldn't help but smile, her heart skipping a little at the sight of it. All it needed was some presents, the fire to be roaring, and some stockings hung off the mantel. Perfect.

It was still light outside, but weary from her activity, Emily pulled out a bargain bin Hallmark Christmas DVD she had bought at the supermarket and slipped the disc into the player. Then, after getting a glass of wine from the fridge, she settled on the sofa for an afternoon of relaxation.

∼

She must have fallen asleep because when she opened her eyes the credits were rolling and it was dark outside the living room window. The curtains were still wide and the tree was gleaming with lights, casting its glow out onto her small front lawn. Outside, the square was dark except for the street lights around the village green and a light through the window of the pub.

Emily sat up, wondering what it was that had woken her, then heard it again, a sharp knock on the door.

She got up, shook the sleep out of her body, then closed the curtains. Out in the hall, she saw the shadow of a face through the frosted glass of the front door.

'Yes?'

'Hello?' came a woman's voice.

'Who is it?'

'Mrs. Taylor from number thirteen, up the road. It's precisely six doors down, not counting the vacant lot where the old scout hut used to stand. So, technically seven, but we wouldn't want to go spoiling things, would we?'

Emily opened the door to reveal an old lady standing there, a beaked nose and crinkly face framed by a rose-like shock of white hair. Her most distinctively quality was of being uncommonly tall for someone so old, at least six feet, so tall that Emily found herself looking upward like a child caught doing something naughty by a teacher.

'Would you like to come in?' Emily asked, aware that a chill wind was gusting, and not too pleased about having it filling her house with cold before she'd managed to get the fire or the heaters going.

'If you don't mind, but I mustn't stop for long. Cameron will be wanting his tea.'

'Come in and sit down. You said you live up the street?'

'Yes, number thirteen. It's unlucky for some, but we can't be biased now, can we?'

'Certainly not. Would you like a cup of tea while I make the fire?'

'That would be nice. It is rather chilly in here. While I applaud you for following this village's sticky rules, there's no need to freeze to death.'

'I fell asleep on the sofa.'

'Napping at your age?' the old lady gave an amused tut. 'What's the world coming to?'

Mrs. Taylor waited patiently for Emily to make tea and then start the fire. Soon, flames were flickering in the hearth, and Mrs. Taylor was entrenched in the armchair, her tea held over her knees.

'You haven't told me your name, dear,' she said, prompting Emily to give her a brief, truncated version of her reason for staying in Cottonwood.

'Well, you could probably have picked somewhere more welcoming,' she said, echoing what Emily had heard elsewhere. 'I mean, us locals are pretty friendly if you can find us, but we've been pushed about so much by all these silly new conditions that those of us not sold up already are thinking to do so. And that's after living here my whole life. Such a shame.'

Sensing an ally, Emily said, 'So you're not here to complain about my tree?'

Mrs. Taylor laughed. 'Oh, I am. But not in the way you might think. I went for my evening walk around the square and noticed you hadn't shut your curtains. I came to tell you to keep it out of sight.'

'Why?'

'Because the parish council—that group of twittering sparrows who somehow got in charge of everything—don't like them. Cottonwood is supposed to be aux naturale, all eco-centric and self-sustaining. However, it's quite clear that no one really cares about anything except for shutting down Christmas.'

'Why would someone do that?'

'Your guess is as good as mine, but since there's only one member of the council who actually lives in Cottonwood, I'd suppose it was his idea.' Mrs. Taylor turned to the fire, as though addressing it directly. 'The insolent little brat.'

'The parish council … aren't they local people?'

'Well, technically. They own properties here, and perhaps show up for a month in the summer to tell everyone else what to do. Cottonwood is popular for second homes. Over half of the houses in the village are owned by people from up country. No one would much care but they've stolen the heart out of the village, they contribute nothing, and yet they like to have a say on how the rest of us live our lives.'

'That's not very nice.'

'We could probably tell them to buzz off, except the biggest snake still lives among us, directing all the gloom-mongering from his doorstep.'

'Trower?'

'Oh, so you've heard about him? It must make you a little uncomfortable.'

'Um, not really. I'm not sure why it would.'

Mrs. Taylor leaned forward. 'Are you certain of that? After all, you're renting one of his properties.'

15

CARNIVAL

AFTER MRS. TAYLOR HAD EXCUSED HERSELF TO GET back to make Cameron's tea, Emily retrieved her newly charged phone and did a little research using a weak connection found only in the upstairs front bedroom. The grumpy but handsome man she was renting a property from was not simply Nathan, but more commonly known as Nathaniel Trower. While there were few details on his personal life, it appeared that Nathan had spent some time working in America as a record producer. Although he was now listed as inactive, in researching his discography, Emily discovered his name behind one of the biggest records of the decade, one which had catapulted its writers to stardom and sold in the region of ten million copies.

Following its release and rise to success, it seemed, Nathan had disappeared into obscurity. The last interviews posted online were dated from 2014, after which the only "new" information she could find was a "Where are there now?" article, which stated that the legendary producer was enjoying an early retirement and had so far refused requests to go back into the studio.

So, Nathan was the archetypal rags-to-riches story. Going off to America, making his fortune, and retiring to his home village.

Where it seemed he had then set himself the task of eradicating Christmas.

Emily rubbed her chin. Something wasn't right.

She switched off her phone, stood up, and went outside, opening her living room curtains before she went.

She did a circuit of the square, sneakily glancing through people's front windows where she could, but in her own was the only place she could see a tree. In fact, true to what Mrs. Taylor had said, less than half the properties appeared occupied, their windows dark, their front lawns grown up. She hadn't brought a torch, but after advancing as far as she dared into the dark, keeping the square's street lights in view behind her, she found most of the larger properties were dark and silent. Only one, the biggest of all on the very outskirts of the village, had a single light on outside, and a glow coming from one of its front windows.

Emily returned to the square. Passing her window with its glittering Christmas tree, she felt suddenly self-conscious, guilty even. She fought the urge to go inside and at the very least draw the curtains, even to pull the plug on the tree lights completely. This was how it had to have happened, she thought. A core group made the decision to effectively cancel Christmas, leaving the rest to slowly talk themselves into compliance. After a couple of years, no one wanted to stand out.

She walked up the other way, toward Veronica's café. In this upper section of the village she found the same as in the lower: of the small percentage of houses which appeared occupied, none had any visible signs of Christmas. It was as though Emily had fallen asleep and woken up at the end of January. Only when she paused at a gateway to look at the lights of a neighbouring village across the valley, the Christmas garden displays of a couple of houses on the outskirts clearly visible even over the distance, did she realise that Cottonwood had become an almost Dickensian Christmas black spot.

'Pretty, aren't they?' came a nearby voice, startling her. Emily gave a little gasp of surprise as she turned to find a middle-aged woman in a jacket and beanie hat standing just a few steps away, her face mostly in shadows cast by the streetlight behind her. In her hands she held a lead, with a little Dachshund snuffling in the grass at the other end.

'Sorry, I didn't mean to startle you.'

'It's all right. I was miles away.'

The woman laughed. 'Wouldn't most of us be, if we could? Sorry, I'm Kelly. Kelly Chambers. I don't believe we've met?'

'Emily Wilson.'

'Ah, I thought so. You're renting one of the lets on the square? You'll probably recognise me better as Peter's mum.'

'Oh, right. You have a lovely lad. He helped me carry some boxes earlier.'

Kelly laughed. 'Oh, he's a love. Always helps me out in the shop. Good as gold. I wish he'd smile a bit more often. He's into all this heavy metal and all that. Seems like being sullen is a pre-requisite.'

'He told me a little about Cottonwood.'

'Yes, he told me he mentioned a few things to you. News travels fast, if you know what I mean. I hear you're almost local anyway?'

'I'm from Birchtide. My grandmother ran Elaine's Teahouse. She passed away in October, and I suppose I'm going through a period of not knowing what to do with everything.'

'It must be tough.'

Emily nodded. 'Tougher than I'd expected. I keep thinking I'll just wake up one morning and everything will have sorted itself out, but it doesn't work like that, does it?'

Kelly shook her head. 'You just have to give it time. Is that why you came here? To get away from things a bit?'

Emily thought about the letter inside her coat. She wasn't yet ready to tell anyone about it, so she just shrugged. 'That's right. Change everything around for a while, but still be within a quick drive of home if I need to rush back.'

'Makes sense. Cottonwood isn't the most lively of places, as I'm sure you've noticed.'

Even though they were clearly alone, the stillness of the air made Emily want to lower her voice. She leaned a little closer as she said, 'Is it true that you're not allowed to have Christmas trees?'

Kelly sighed. 'You've picked up on the rules then?

You're allowed a tree, you're just not supposed to put lights on it. The parish council actually voted on it. Only later did we all find out that nine of the ten council members don't even live here for more than a month a year, and the chairman is holed up in his gloomy mansion at the end of the village, miles away from everyone else.'

'Can't you all just ignore it?'

Kelly shrugged. 'There aren't enough strong personalities around to stand up to it. No one wants to risk any petty retribution. It came into effect two years ago. Three people said screw it, and put trees up with all the usual lights, just to annoy the lord in his manor over there. One of them ended up with a potato stuffed in his car exhaust. The second was Alan, over at Rowe Farm. For the next month his gates were mysteriously opening by themselves, and his livestock kept getting out. And the third had her suppliers all cancelled after they all received a mysterious letter informing them of the business's closure.'

'You?'

Kelly nodded. 'Yep. I put up a tree inside the store. We were closed over the Christmas period, but when we reopened, none of my deliveries showed up. It took a couple of weeks of phone calls and explaining to sort it all out. By then I'd lost several regular customers who had specific orders. Round here, you have to keep the locals sweet. They're your bread and butter.'

'My grandmother would have agreed with that.'

'And once they're gone, it's a nightmare trying to bring them back.'

'So you think this Trower guy was behind it?'

'Oh, so you've heard about him, have you? No one likes to say his name, because it feels like he's always listening.'

'I found out a couple of hours ago that I was renting from him. Having met him, I find it hard to believe. I mean, he's so….'

'Handsome?' Kelly grinned. 'Oh, gosh, has he been the fantasy at some point for every local girl over the age of fifteen. He looks like he's stepped out of a fashion catalogue, doesn't he?'

Emily felt like an idiot as she said, 'I couldn't look away. Even though he came across as kind of a git, it only made it worse.'

'With his looks, he should be grinning from ear to ear all day long,' Kelly said. 'He's loaded, too. His family was already pretty well off, but he went to America, worked in the music business, and came out on top. He had the world at his feet, but for some reason he decided to come back here, hide away in that big old house and buy up everything that came on the market.'

'What do you mean?'

'Didn't you know? He's the biggest landowner round here. He owns seven houses in the village, and they're all empty most of the year. He lets them in the summer months, but the rest of the year they're vacant.'

'He said something about forgetting to take mine off the market.'

'That would make sense. It feels like he's squeezing the life out of Cottonwood. Quite a few locals want to leave, but they're not prepared to sell their houses to Nathaniel Trower.'

'Couldn't they make it an exclusion of some kind?'

'Some tried. Once he offered forty percent over the asking price, and the chap couldn't say no. Another place was bought by a company, which turned out to be Trower under an alias. He's a sneaky one. Being chairman of the parish council, he has his fingers in the pocket of the County Council too. When public land gets sold off, he's the first in there. He bought a couple of old bridleways without the sales even going public. Caused terrible trouble for poor Alan Rowe. Made him relocate a couple of field gates for his cows. Alan wanted to go to court to fight for access, but he doesn't have the time or money to dispute it.'

Emily thought about the kind farmer and how welcome she had felt in his home. The thought of someone doing something so unkind to such a nice man, particularly one forced by unfortunate circumstances to bring up two children on his own, made her feel a knot of anger in her stomach.

'That's awful.'

Kelly nodded. 'But the worst for the rest of us is what happened to the village green. It used to be public land. Then, two years ago, the County Council decided to sell it off. Trower bought it before anyone knew it was on the market. The very first thing he did was cancel our yearly Christmas carnival.'

16

MEMORIES

Emily hadn't noticed Cottonwood Village Hall before, but after her conversation the night before with Kelly Chambers, she walked up through the village, past Veronica's café and found it down a lane almost missable between two overgrown hedgerows.

At the end of the lane, a gravel car park was strewn with weeds. The hall was a ramshackle barn of a building with a faded sign hung from patchy walls desperately in need of a coat of paint. Overgrown hedgerows hemmed it in on three sides, but on the fourth a grassy field dotted with decrepit children's play apparatus sloped down to a low stone wall separating it from a pasture field. A view opened out of the valley below, the buildings of a neighbouring village visible in the distance, as though to taunt the village hall of better things.

Inside a covered porch, the minutes of the last council meeting were posted inside a plastic file pinned up on a cork noticeboard. Other notices, for various social events such as a badminton club, a twice monthly coffee morning, and a film club, looked hopelessly out of date.

The main door was unlocked, as Kelly had claimed it would be ('They lost the key and somehow can't find the funds in the budget to replace it'), so Emily slipped inside and found herself standing in a gloomy high-ceilinged room. Blinds hung down over the windows, and when she tried the lights, she found three of the six overhead ceiling lights were in need of new bulbs. Two were completely dead, while a third flickered incessantly, causing so much irritation that eventually she switched it off.

The windows needed a clean. Some of the tramlines for a badminton court were ripped and curled upward. Two chairs with broken legs were stacked in a corner, and when Emily reached down to touch the floor, her finger came away with a layer of dust.

At the far end of the main room was a little stage with doors to either side. One led through into a toilet and storage area, the other into a small library with a connected kitchen. Emily remembered what Kelly had told her and went to the local history section of the library, where she found a line of professionally made photograph books beginning in 1980. She pulled one out and looked at the front.

"A Pictorial Memory of Cottonwood Parish, 1987."

The book was filled with glossy colour photographs of the previous year, all annotated.

There was the summer carnival, local parish walks, history lectures, barn dances, concerts, and there at the end, Cottonwood Christmas Carnival, held on the village green over the last weekend before Christmas.

Emily put the book back and took another from a few years later. It was the same kind of thing, a series of local events culminating in the Christmas carnival. She looked at a few, and in one picture from 2008 recognised what appeared to be a young Veronica and Peter dressed up as reindeer. Two years later there was a picture of a youthful Kelly with her thumbs up from behind a stall selling mince pies, the year after that Alan grinning over a huge, steaming turkey. Mrs. Taylor had even made it into that shot, holding a Yorkshire Terrier with its paw raised as she grinned for the camera.

The last book was dated 2016. There were no others.

Emily frowned. She had thought how well the village seemed suited to a carnival of some kind, and her hunch had been right. However, over the past couple of years a malaise had fallen over Cottonwood, and its name was Nathaniel Trower. Karen would certainly tell her to bail, to get out of the village and hurry over to David's family mansion for a *National Lampoon* Christmas. Elaine, however, would want to fix things. Emily's grandmother had hated to see anyone not enjoying themselves, and Emily had inadvertently stumbled upon an entire village suffering from an absence of joy.

That the cause appeared to be Emily's landlord was something she would have to deal with in time.

Walking away was not an option, not now she had found something to finally draw her mind away from her grief. Cottonwood felt like a project, one which would take a great effort to complete, but one of which Elaine would greatly approve.

She put the book back and returned to the entrance to read over the council meeting notes again.

The last meeting had been on the second of December. Five councilors had apologised for their absence. Four others had joined via video call. Only one had actually shown up in person, and that one was Nathaniel Trower.

Emily frowned. The council setup didn't sit right. Elaine had been on Birchtide's parish council for as long as Emily could remember, and her grandmother had talked about certain rules. New members had to be voted in by the existing, and a certain amount of attendance was required otherwise you forfeited your spot. Taking out her phone, she took a picture of the minutes, intending to do some more research later.

The sky was clear and the early morning breeze had died away, leaving a pleasant day for walking. Emily left the village hall behind and continued walking until she had gone past the outskirts of the village, surrounding herself with farmland dipping away into forested valleys. She passed several stiles leading to public access footpaths, some with interesting signs such as "Towbridge Waterfall" and "Hawker Old Mill". Had she worn better shoes she might have challenged one, but being unfamiliar with the routes, she felt it better if she had some companionship.

She had met a few people around the village, but there was no one she yet considered a friend. Friendship, however, was something that needed to be cultivated. Like a flower, Elaine had often said. If you ignore it, it'll fade away and die, but if you water it regularly, it'll surely bloom.

Most people didn't need watering, of course, but there was another way to get their attention, and Emily, thanks to Elaine, was a master at it.

Food.

And in particular, cakes.

17

UNWANTED VISITOR

She hadn't planned to use the holiday let as a cooking factory, so she went over to Peter's shop and stocked up on what she could, before jumping in the car and heading to the nearest supermarket to pick up what she couldn't. When she returned in late afternoon, her car was laden with baking trays, bags of flour and sugar, butter, spices, and tins of dried fruit and nuts.

With only a pause to find a station playing Christmas songs on the old radio, she got straight to work, turning the kitchen into a production line of cakes, tarts, and biscuits. By the time she looked up to find that the sun had set and night had fallen, several airing trays were piled high with mince pies, Eccles cakes, treacle tarts, sponge cakes, and caramel shortcakes. Elaine, as her strength and energy had begun to fail her, had passed off all her recipes and cooking methods to Emily, eventually passing on the majority of the cooking duty to her granddaughter while she manned the shop front. However, by insisting on tasting everything, Elaine ensured Emily had baked to a high standard. Now, as she surveyed her handiwork, she found herself grinning at the memory of her grandmother standing over her, holding a piece of caramel shortcake in her hands and frowning, before saying, 'Hmm, let me try a little bit more. It needs to make me feel just shy of a heart attack before it's perfect.'

'Miss you,' Emily said, as she had so often, washing her hands before going to the fridge and pulling out her unfinished bottle of wine. It was time for a celebratory drink.

She put on her jacket and went out to the back patio. The air was still but the temperature had dropped with the departing sun, so Emily found herself shivering as she watched her Christmas illumination blinking on.

Within a few minutes, all of the lights had illuminated, brightening the garden right down to the bottom fence. She wondered how easily she could shift the picnic table down onto the lawn in order to accommodate a Christmas party. Elaine had loved Christmas parties on the back terrace, some of them private invite only for her favourite customers and a few friends, where they were treated like guinea pigs for her new creations. Emily wondered if she could cobble together enough locals for a decent party, then remembered the pictures of the Christmas carnival she had seen.

They were out there somewhere. Like fossils, they were lying dormant, waiting to be rediscovered.

The night was almost quiet, only the occasional hoot of an owl echoing across the valley or the distant rumble of a car. Emily finished her wine and was about to head inside when a strange buzzing sound came from somewhere overhead, beyond the gardens to her left. The noise grew as something came closer, a high-speed whirring which sounded strangely familiar. She frowned, trying to recall where she had heard such a sound before.

The sound intensified before fading again, as if whatever was making it was moving quickly, but not following any regular route, rather shooting back and forth as though it couldn't decide where to go.

Birchtide Public Park, that was it. A man helping a young boy test out his birthday present.

A drone.

She stood up, peering up into the sky, wondering if it was right above her. Who on earth would be flying one at this time of night, and what on earth would they be hoping to see?

She had no experience of them other than seeing a couple buzzing around in the sky, but weren't they mostly used for taking videos and photographs of scenery? That, or….

She shook her head. No. It had to be someone taking pictures of the stars or something. They couldn't possibly be spying.

It sounded right overhead. If they were watching the stars, it wouldn't matter, because the camera would be facing a different direction, but just in case it was someone spying on her, she waved her hands at it, then crossed them over each other, mouthing at the same time—just in case its camera was good enough to make it out—'Go away.'

For a few seconds the sound hung there above her before slowly fading as the machine retreated. Emily tried to figure out where it had gone, but her ears weren't the best and the wind chose exactly the wrong time to offer a solid gust, as though to remind her that winter was here. By the time it had died away, so had the whir of the drone's propellers.

Emily took her wine glass and went back inside, washing it in the sink. Despite the gorgeous aroma of freshly cooked cakes, the drone's appearance had soured her mood somewhat. Perhaps it had been some local kid playing around with a toy while his parents were watching TV unawares.

Or perhaps not.

18

SABOTAGE

Monday morning brought a miserable deluge of rain. Emily watched with dismay as it battered the village square outside, turning the gravel parking area into a field of puddles. Hoping that it cleared by the afternoon, she decided instead on a trip back to the teahouse to check the post. The electric and gas bills had shown up, as well as another handful of Christmas cards. Not wanting to stay in the teahouse but not in the mood to return to Cottonwood just yet, she drove to a café a couple of miles away where she had sometimes met with friends on days when she needed a break from the teahouse's endless hustle and bustle.

She took a corner seat, ordered a latte and began opening Christmas cards. She was barely halfway through, finding cards from a few distant relatives perhaps unaware of Elaine's passing but mostly from customers, when she heard footsteps approaching her table.

'Emily Wilson? Is that you? Is this where you've been hiding?'

Emily looked up into the face of an overdressed middle-aged woman so overburdened with mascara that she was only a couple of brush strokes short of a circus. Emily couldn't recall her name but remembered seeing her in the teahouse from time to time, usually in the company of a group of similarly dressed older upper-class types.

'Hello?' she said.

'I must say, how much longer are you going to keep us all waiting?'

'Um, for what?'

'For your grandmother's cakes, that's what. There are people out there practically dying of starvation while you sit in here opening Christmas cards.'

Emily couldn't help but smile. She considered mentioning that there were enough to fill half of Birchtide sitting on the counter in her holiday let, but thought better of it.

'I'm not sure,' she said.

'You're letting people down, you know. Elaine's passing was a terrible thing, but letting that place sit empty … you're soiling her memory.'

At the woman's abrupt change of tone, Emily wrinkled her nose, resisting the urge to say something harsh. No matter how loved her grandmother had been, no one had loved her more than Emily.

'I'm just sorting through a few things. Please be patient.'

'You'll lose your regulars, you know,' the woman said. Then, with a surreptitious glance around the inside of the café, she added in a quieter tone, 'Well, you would if there was anywhere else worth going round here. Come on, dear, we're waiting for you to save us from café purgatory.'

And with that, and a dramatic sweep of her coat, the woman was gone.

Emily stared after her, picking at the remains of her words, wondering which bits had been truth and which an embellished exaggeration.

When she next went to take a sip from her latte, she found it had gone cold. She packed away her things and went out to the car. It was still raining, but it had eased off to an extent that it just made you soggy instead of soaking you right through. She switched on the engine then sat staring through the rain blotting the windscreen, wondering what to do. Without doubt, the old woman wasn't alone in wanting the teahouse open again. Emily just didn't know if she had the heart.

She called Karen.

'Hello, my lovely,' Karen said. 'We're just in the middle of a game of Monopoly. David's dad has everything except Mayfair and Oxford Street. You can see how he made his money. What are you up to?'

'I'm sitting in the car in a rainy car park in the middle of nowhere, wondering what to do with the rest of my life.'

'Well, have you had lunch yet?'

'Not yet.'

'There's the next hour sorted. Get yourself filled up first. Then take it from there. No one thinks straight on an empty stomach. Shall I get David to ask the butler—I can't believe he has a butler!—to make up a spare room for you?'

'No, it's fine. I'm just moping. If it would stop raining and start snowing I might feel better.'

'David said some's forecast for next week. Hang in there.'

'I'll do my best.'

'And remember—'

'I know, I know. I'll be in touch when my life starts falling apart again.'

'I'll keep the phone nearby after lunch.'

'Thanks.'

'Hang in there. Things will work out. Just trust me.'

Emily smiled as she hung up. Talking to Karen always made her feel better, but as soon as the call was over she was thrust back into the reality of her own loneliness. Twenty-nine years old and alone in the world. Elaine had provided a buffer for far longer than she should have, and the teahouse had offered her a false shield of sociality. As much as the warmth and chatter of the teahouse had mattered to her, however, the inhabitants had been customers and acquaintances, not true friends, and Elaine had been the mastermind of it all.

With her grandmother gone, Emily felt like a chocolate egg lying in the middle of a motorway, minus its wrapper, waiting to be crushed.

She tilted her head, looking at herself in the rearview mirror. 'Who am I?' she whispered, wondering if she was really going through an existential crisis or whether it was just rainy day blues brought on by the onset of a lonely Christmas, all collected together in the fishing net of her overburdening grief.

She forced a smile then gave herself a little slap on the cheek.

'Snap out of it,' she said. 'Those cakes won't deliver themselves.'

She headed back to Cottonwood. By the time she had reached the village, the rain had passed over and ragged diamonds of blue had appeared between the clouds. It looked like being a nice afternoon.

Before going back to the holiday let, she went into the shop, where she found Kelly Chambers behind the counter. As Peter's mum wished Emily a good afternoon, a bark came from a basket tucked in next to a rack of magazines. A dog climbed up and came ambling over to sniff at Emily's feet. It looked up at her, barked once more, wagged its tail, and then returned to its bed.

'Looks like Rudolph remembers you.'

'Rudolph?'

Kelly smiled. 'Peter chose it. We got him Rudolph for Christmas when he was twelve. Yeah, I know you're not supposed to get children pets, but we were fully prepared to look after him if Peter was more interested in computer games. Luckily they got on okay, although I have to do most of the walking duties these days.'

'It's a nice name.'

'Christmassy. I like it best at this time of year, although these days it's a little bittersweet.'

'I saw the pictures of the Christmas carnival. It looked lovely.'

'It was. It was the village's main event. It still would be if Trower wasn't such a Scrooge.'

'Can't you hold it somewhere else?'

Kelly shrugged. 'I don't know. I mean, I suppose it's possible. It's just that no one wants to organise it, nor risk Trower's wrath. He's a powerful man in Cottonwood.'

'So I keep hearing. I don't think it's fair that he gets to dictate whether or not the rest of you enjoy yourselves.'

'Well, if you decide to take him on, let me know. I want a front row ticket.'

Emily picked up a couple of things for lunch before wishing Kelly a good afternoon and heading back across the road to the holiday let. As she let herself in the door, however, her nerves immediate pricked up. Something felt wrong. The house was colder than it should have been, the air fresher, the smell of cooked cakes and pies less pervading than it had been when she left. She took off her shoes and hurried down the hall to the kitchen.

As she opened the door, something black fluttered away from the kitchen counter. Emily let out a gasp of surprise, jumping back as the crow fled through the open back door. It wasn't the only one, she found, as she stepped through the entrance, waving her hands to shoo off the others. Four, five, six, she counted, before she managed to get the back door shut.

She turned around, and let out another gasp, this one of horror. The birds had made a mess of her cakes, tucking into the ones she had left uncovered. While the mince pies, Eccles cakes, and one treacle tart were safe inside plastic containers she had found in a cupboard under the sink, a sponge cake she had left under a thin piece of gauze to "mature", as Elaine would have called it, had been decimated. Similar destruction had been wreaked on a pecan pie, while a cheesecake had been cleared of the expensive out-of-season strawberries she had clustered on the top, the rest of it left clawed and mangled. One corner even dribbled with grey-brown crow poop.

Growling with frustration, she set about clearing up the mess and throwing away the ruined cakes. Elaine had sometimes left the back door open to let her fresh cakes get a little air, but Emily was certain she had closed it. Unless she was losing her mind.

The cleanup operation over, she retreated to the living room with a glass of wine. Too tired to start the fire, she glared into yesterday's embers, trying to convince herself that it hadn't been her fault the door was open and the crows had got in.

She was certain she had, if not locked it, then at least closed it. The door was old, a little loose-fitting, but it couldn't have slipped open, surely?

Perhaps she ought to call the police. Someone might have broken in while she was out, sensing the rich pickings of someone on holiday. However, she had left her laptop on a kitchen surface, and it was still there, untouched. Nothing else appeared to have been disturbed.

Maybe someone else had come in. A cleaner perhaps?

She put her wine down and went upstairs. Her bed, hastily made this morning, looked the same. Her towel was hung over the landing stair rail where she had left it.

Not a cleaner then.

Perhaps the landlord had paid her a visit? After all, he would certainly have a spare key.

Nathan. Nathaniel Trower. The village Scrooge, hell-bent on ruining Christmas for everyone.

She started thinking about the drone from last night. What if Trower was spying on her, and leaving her back door open for the crows to get in was deliberate sabotage attempt to get back at her for flaunting the village's rules about Christmas decorations?

Emily went back downstairs. She had taken her boots off before coming in the door, leaving them in the small covered porch, but as she leaned down to touch the doormat just inside the main door, her fingers came away damp.

Someone had been inside, leaving their shoes here while they looked around.

She might not be able to prove it to the police, but there was no doubt in Emily's mind what had happened.

Elaine had possessed the heart of a saint, but she had got to her status in life by possessing a steel core. When hard decisions had to be made, she made them. And she had never backed down from a challenge.

It was time for Emily to channel her

grandmother's spirit and confront the local Krampus over both his actions and his attitude. He might be able to push around a few poor locals, but Emily wasn't standing for it.

What Nathaniel Trower had done could not be ignored.

19

CONFRONTATION

Nathaniel Trower's house had three storeys from what Emily could see as she made her way down the driveway with a bag slung over her shoulder. It looked like a cross between a farmhouse and a gothic mansion, stone walls topped with little ornamental parapets and fake battlements. There was even a tower room, from which she imagined the views were impressive.

The driveway swung around to the left, ending in a wide turning circle. The door was in a gloomy covered porch, giving the impression of walking into a cave. Emily knocked on the door then stepped back until she was standing outside on the drive, as though afraid the door might open to reveal a portal sucking her into a maelstrom of darkness.

It was an age before anyone answered. There was no sign of the dogs Nathan had mentioned, and Emily was about to give up when an intercom beside the door, which she hadn't even noticed, gave a tired, flat-battery beep, and a crackly voice said, 'What is it?'

'It's Emily Wilson. I'm staying in your property just up the road? I just brought you round a present. Can I come in?'

'I'm busy right now.'

She gave her sweetest smile, aware that a camera was probably hidden in the gloom. 'It'll only be a minute. I've brought you a cake, but I wanted to explain the best way to eat it.'

'Thanks. Can't you just leave it on the step?'

Emily shook her head. 'I saw something in your garden. I think it might have been a rat or a squirrel. They're pretty hungry at this time of the year. If you're busy I don't mind waiting.'

She pulled out her phone and pretended to browse the internet, making it clear she was going nowhere until the door opened.

'All right. Just wait a minute.'

He made her wait. Despite his looks, Emily could understand why he was single. He clearly had no idea how to treat a girl, but perhaps in his profession and with his wealth, that hadn't mattered.

The door finally opened and Nathan stepped out. Emily's knees immediately weakened, and she wished her heart would pay more attention to her head. He was hopelessly attractive in a black roll-neck sweater and blue jeans, both hugging a figure which was lean and powerful. His jaw jutted like the prow of an icebreaker, his eyes the turquoise of a radioactive lake.

'What do you want? I was in the middle of something.'

Emily held up the box. 'I did some cooking the other day and I brought you something to say thank you for your hospitality. I'm having a lovely time. I'm so glad you forgot to take your properties off the website.'

Nathan looked taken aback. He blinked, then gave a slight shake of his head. 'Oh, well, that's good I suppose.'

'Cottonwood is just delightful, and the locals are so friendly. I really wish I lived around here.' Emily stopped herself before she could vomit up a bunch of spiel about Christmas spirit, afraid of overdoing it.

'I'm glad you're having a good time.'

'Well, let's have tea, shall we? Do you have any fresh cream?' She stepped under the porch roof and began to remove her boots.

'Ah, I don't know—'

'That's fine. I brought some.'

'Well, I suppose you ought to come in then.'

Nathan stepped back inside. Emily hurried past him before he could change his mind, finding herself in a gloomy but well-kept house with an abundance of fine furniture but a complete absence of any clutter. She felt like she was walking into a vintage show home, any signs of any personal touch hidden from sight.

'You don't have any dogs then?'

'What?'

'You said you had dogs. You said not to ring late or they'd go mental and annoy the old bag next door.'

'Oh. They, um, died.'

'All of them?'

'Uh, yes.'

'And I suppose there's no old bag next door?'

Nathan gave a noncommittal shrug. 'I haven't seen her in a while, so I couldn't say for sure.'

'Perhaps you just don't like the sound of the phone?'

'It gives me headaches.'

'Yet you were a record producer?'

'I—'

Emily flashed him a grin not quite genuine enough to make it obvious whether or not she was joking, then, without being asked, went down a long hall into a wide lounge-diner with views over an extensive sloping lawn. A copy of The Times lay open on a dining table, a cup of coffee steaming beside it.

'Oh, the kettle must still be hot. I'd love one,' Emily said. 'White, no sugar.'

'Right. Okay.'

Nathan went into an adjoining kitchen. As soon as he was out of sight, Emily grabbed the back of the nearest chair and forced herself to take a few long, slow breaths. She had gained entry, now she had to take control of the situation.

A couple of minutes later, Nathan returned with a mug of coffee. He took a placemat from out of a holder on a side shelf and put it down on the tabletop before handing Emily the mug. As she took a sip, he glanced at the newspaper, as though hoping she would soon leave.

'You have a lovely house,' Emily said. 'Is it just you?'

'Yes. My father has passed away. My mother lives in a care home in Brighton.'

'Oh, such a long way away.'

'My sister cares for her.'

'Right. So you have a sister?'

'One. Younger.'

Emily pursed her lips. 'Do you visit often?'

'No.'

Nathan retrieved the remains of his coffee and stared out of the window while he drank it. Emily got the distinct impression that he didn't like being around people. Well, tough. If you destroyed someone's cakes, you might as well have cut off one of their feet, as Elaine might have said.

'So, would you like to see what I brought you?'

Nathan shrugged. 'Sure.'

Emily took the box out of her bag and set it down on the table. Then, with a smile, she lifted the lid.

Nathan took a step back, his body shuddering. 'Get that thing out of here.'

'What's the matter?'

'I mean it. Right now.'

He had clenched his fists and lifted them out to the sides of his face like a child preparing to throw a toy. His face, so naturally handsome, had contorted into an expression of rage coupled with disgust.

And something else, hidden in his eyes.

Fear.

Emily looked down at the little Christmas cake, with its jolly Father Christmas figurine standing next to a grinning snowman. It wasn't quite as good as the supermarket ones, but she had added a few swirls of icing to give it a personal touch, and was really quite proud of it.

'Now!' he shouted, eyes wide, practically hyperventilating. 'Get it out of my house!'

Emily scooped up the cake as Nathan's hand came swinging down, swiping it out of his reach before he could dash it to the floor. He growled, gripping his face with his hands as she retreated down the hall toward the front door.

'I'm sorry, perhaps this was a bad time—'

'Out!'

She didn't wait for him to come and see her off. She slipped on her boots and fled down the driveway, out through the gate onto the road. Only when she was well clear of Trower's house did she pause to get her breath back.

Of all the reactions she had expected, that had not been one of them. Nathan hadn't just been angry at the sight of the Christmas cake. He had been terrified.

He didn't just dislike Christmas.

It haunted him.

20

DELIVERIES

'All right? Still here then?'

Veronica sounded almost pleased to see Emily, even though the briefest hint of a smile was a blink-and-miss-it event. As Emily came inside, Veronica lifted a mug.

'Brew?'

'Yes, please.'

'What you been up to?'

Emily smiled. 'I went to see Nathaniel Trower. I took him round a Christmas cake, but he … didn't want it.'

'No?'

Emily put the box down on the counter and lifted the lid. 'Am I missing something? Is there something scary about this?'

Veronica looked over. 'Pretty. Ha, the Father Christmas is a bit wonky. Could be drunk, eh.'

'I just ran up the street. I almost dropped it.'

'You want to be more careful.'

'I'll try.'

Veronica made the tea while Emily cut out two thick slices of the cake and put them onto plates.

'Trower threw me out of his house,' Emily said. 'I showed him the cake and he went off on one.'

Veronica shrugged. 'Well, he is a bit mental. Lives up in that big house on his own, hates Christmas.'

'Any idea why?'

'Nope.'

'I thought maybe he was just mean, but he looked terrified. Like I'd shoved a bug in his face.'

'Caterpillars.'

'What?'

'Caterpillars. Hate them. That would do it for me. You shove a caterpillar in my face and I'll stab you with one of these sticks.'

'Is that what they're there for?'

'Nope. Saw it in a magazine. Looked cool. Feels a bit weird but you get used to it.'

Emily smiled. 'Anyway, feel free to sell the rest of this cake. Have you had any customers in yet today?'

'Yeah, one.'

'That's great. Who?'

'You.'

Emily laughed. Veronica even offered a smile. 'Well, it's a start.'

'I made up some new menus like you said.' Veronica lifted up a sheet of laminated paper. 'Looks better, doesn't it?'

Emily nodded as she took the paper and looked over its contents. 'Much better,' she said. 'It's clearer, only sells what you've actually got in stock, and looks pretty as well.'

'Thanks. Did it myself on the computer.'

'You did a good job. Have you thought about anything else I said?'

Veronica nodded. 'Yeah. Customers now get a free glass of water with whatever they order.'

Emily cocked her head. 'Is that right? Where's mine?'

'You have to ask for it, don't you?'

'Just put it on their table when they sit down. If they say they didn't order it, tell them it's free and to ask if they want a refill.'

'Right. But what if they don't order anything? Can't have people sitting there all day drinking tap water.'

'With a menu like this and a rack of cakes sitting over there, how could they not?'

Veronica frowned as though processing this, then nodded. 'Right.'

'If you've not got anything going on tomorrow, why don't I come over and show you a few recipes?'

'Yeah? Thanks.'

'And you might want to think about getting some Christmas decorations up in the window.'

'But what about Trower? He might slag me off online or something. Won't get any customers then.'

'I'll deal with Trower.'

'How?'

Emily thought for a moment. She wasn't quite sure what she would do, only that she couldn't let the stagnation she had found in Cottonwood carry on any longer.

'I'm going to figure him out,' she said.

∽

Half an hour later, after briefly popping back home, she walked through the door of the Inn on the Green and found Skip sitting on a stool behind the counter, watching a wildlife documentary on the TV hung over the bar.

'Hi there. Didn't you come in the other day?'

Emily smiled. 'That's right. Emily.'

Skip clicked his fingers. 'That's it. I heard from her in the shop that you were staying for a couple of weeks. Over in one of Trower's lets, aren't you?'

'Much to his dismay,' Emily said. 'I think he might try to kick me out pretty soon.'

'Why's that? He's all right as long as you leave him alone.'

'And don't mention Christmas,' Emily said. 'I took him round a cake, you know, just to be nice. He threw me out of his house.'

Skip grunted with surprise. 'Well, next time you're handing out cakes, don't bother with him, just bring them over here.'

Emily pulled a box out of her bag and put it down on the bar. 'Da-da,' she said, lifting off the lid. 'Mince pies. Homemade.'

Skip looked like a kid waking up on his first Christmas morning. He stared at the box with such undisguised excitement that Emily couldn't help but laugh.

'Save some for your customers.'

'Really? Can't I just close up?'

'Christmas is a time for sharing, Skip.'

The old man rolled his eyes. 'Only if anyone comes in. If not, they're mine.'

'Sounds like a good deal. If you want more, anytime. I've not got much else to do for the next couple of weeks other than wander around the village and cook stuff.'

Skip narrowed his eyes. 'What are you, some kind of Christmas fairy?'

'Not quite. Actually, I wanted to ask you something.'

'Sure.'

'Cottonwood used to have a Christmas carnival. I know it used to be over on the green, but it seems that your resident wet blanket has put a dampener on that. I was wondering where else you could organise one.'

Skip looked uncertain. 'Are you sure you want to get involved in something like that? You'd be risking Trower's wrath.'

'I've already seen him at his worst.'

'You think? He's a powerful man. I wouldn't want to get his back up.'

'I was brought up by a woman who would take any bully to the cleaners, give them a good dunking, then bring them back and give them coffee and a cake. I'm not scared of Trower or anyone else.'

'Well, let me know how it goes.'

'Thanks, I will. Just for argument's sake, if I could

get enough people together interested in setting up an event, is there somewhere here where we could meet?'

Skip smiled. 'The Smuggler's Room.'

'The what?'

'It's the private bar, round the back. It used to be used for weddings and other functions, but there aren't enough people round here anymore for those kind of things to happen. If you get a group together, let me know, and I'll stock the bar.'

'That would be great. At the moment it's you and me.'

'I never said I'd be involved—'

'You'd be guilty by association.'

Skip looked pained. 'Look, if you can find the interest, count me in. Getting one over on Trower would be the best Christmas present ever. You've got to get a good group, though, otherwise there won't be enough people to split his wrath.'

Emily nodded. 'Deal,' she said, reaching out to shake Skip's hand. 'Now, if you'll excuse me, I have some more deliveries to make.'

21

DIRT AND BACKHANDERS

To Emily's delight, when she emerged from the pub she found it had started to snow. Clouds had drifted in to fill the sky and as the sun dipped behind the hedgerows to the west the first flakes began to settle on the ground. Quickly returning to the holiday let—and making doubly sure that the doors and windows were locked this time—she set out again, a bag under one arm and a torch held in her free hand.

The road to Rowe Farm wasn't nearly as imposing with a light to guide her, although to be fair she took the shorter route heading left around the church, rather than the right-hand fork which had taken her through forest. Twenty minutes after setting out, she turned into Alan's driveway, finding a single outside light illuminating the farmyard.

Emily's knock was answered by Lily, whose face lit up at the sight of her standing out in the dark with a box under her arm. She grabbed Emily's torch hand

and pulled her inside, barely giving Emily time to slip off her shoes.

John was in the living room, watching TV. He looked up, a sullen expression immediately clearing as he gave her a little wave, before vanishing as though he considered expressions of happiness an insult to his oncoming teenage years.

Alan, it seemed, was still out in the yard. Lily introduced Emily to an elderly lady called Mrs. Williams ('please call me Barbara'), an old family friend who minded the children while Alan was still at work.

Barbara made Emily a cup of tea, but before Emily could explain why she had come, Lily had dragged her upstairs to play. For the next hour they dressed, fed, bathed, hospitalised and recuperated Lily's farm animals, before a light knock on the bedroom door announced Alan's return.

'Barbara told me you were here,' Alan said with a smile. 'Lily, is it okay if I borrow Emily for a few minutes?'

'Only if I can have her back later.'

Alan shrugged at Emily. 'You'll have to ask her nicely, won't you?' he told his daughter.

'It would be my pleasure,' Emily said. 'I just need to talk to your dad first.'

'Well, okay then.' Lily let out an exaggerated sigh.

Downstairs, the tea Barbara had made had long gone cold, so Alan set the kettle boiling again then offered Emily a seat at the table. He had already showered and changed, she noticed, his hair and beard shining like a shampoo advert, a few spots of perspiration on his brow, and while she couldn't be certain, it appeared he had even trimmed his beard back a little.

He pointed to the box. 'Thank you so much for the treacle tart,' he said. 'I couldn't help but take a little peek. It looks delicious.'

'Just a little thank-you for helping me the other day.'

'It was nothing. How has your stay been?'

Even had Emily not heard from Kelly about Trower's alleged sabotage missions against those villagers who dared celebrate Christmas, she would still have felt comfortable telling Alan what had been going on. His demeanour had a certain warmth about it, a projection of safety. Whatever she told him would stay between them.

'Not the best, to be honest,' she said, then explained about finding the door open, before going on to say what had happened at Trower's house.

'I mean, I know he did it. He's the only one likely to have a key unless he's given one to the cleaner, and it was probably an attempt to punish me for putting the decorations up in the garden. Instead of going round and ranting at him, I wanted to see if I could get him to confess. But … nope. It's like he has a real hatred for Christmas. I mean, I've only been here a few days, but everything else that's going on seems like just foundations for this. For stopping people from enjoying Christmas.'

Alan nodded along with what she was saying, his fingers occasionally drumming on the tabletop. He handed her a cup of tea as she finished, then gave a long sigh.

'You're an astute one,' he said. 'You picked up in a couple of days what it took us months to figure out. It's the reason he bought up all those properties, not to mention the village green.'

'Do you have any idea why?'

Alan shook his head. 'We were in school together, but he was three or four years below me, so I hardly knew him. I'd nod and say hello if I saw him about the village, but we didn't hang out. He was a bit odd. Some of us used to wander about, getting into mischief, the usual kid stuff, but he would always stay at home. He was quiet, a bit aloof. Girls loved him, but he never seemed interested.'

'It's so strange. His reaction to my cake was pure disgust. I've never known anyone to outright hate Christmas.'

Alan shook his head. 'I can't give you an answer, I'm afraid. We used to be on the same school bus, but he always sat down the front on his own. I think there were Christmas parties at school, but I don't recall if he was there, or what he did. He was never at the Christmas carnivals held on the green, but then he wasn't part of my circle of friends, so I wouldn't have hung out with him even if he was. He can't have liked it though, or he wouldn't have bought up the village green and shut down the event.'

Emily grimaced. 'The thing is … he didn't. Buy the green, I mean.'

'What are you talking about?'

'I wondered how he had managed to buy up

public land so easily, so I made a few phone calls. It turns out that he hasn't bought it at all. He's spinning everyone in the village a complete line.'

Alan frowned. 'But there was an official contract posted in the village hall. I've seen it.'

'It's not real. Neither are these so-called parish councillors. I looked them up online, or tried to. At least five of them don't exist. A couple of others are just names of people who own properties in Cottonwood. I called two of them. They had no idea they were even on the parish council. Trower is playing the entire village for a fool.'

Alan tugged on his beard. 'I feel so foolish … I remember we had a private meeting about the green in the pub a couple of weeks after that message was posted. Someone contacted the council about it and we were told there was nothing we could do.'

'You were probably fed a lie in return for some backhander. Trower probably has a mate on the county council. Luckily, so do I, and I know without doubt that my contact is trustworthy because I've been dealing with him for years.'

Alan cocked his head. 'Who exactly are you, Emily? You just appear out of nowhere with a mission to save Christmas for the residents of Cottonwood. Are you sure you're not one of Trower's other mates here to get our hopes up?'

Emily smiled. 'I'm the granddaughter of a woman who knew business inside out,' she said. 'Unfortunately, as she got older, she was less able to handle everything, so much of it got passed on to me.'

Only as she said it did she realise how much it was

true. She had always thought of herself as the elf to Elaine's Father Christmas, busy and industrious but still little more than a shadow. Now, as she thought back over the last few years, she realised that Elaine had been grooming her, passing off her decades of knowledge piece by piece, preparing Emily for the time when her grandmother would no longer be around.

'I think I'll go and sharpen my pitchfork,' Alan said.

'Excuse me?'

'For when we march on Trower's castle to overthrow the local feudal lord.'

'I wasn't suggesting—'

Alan grinned. 'I'm joking. However, while I agree with you that something has to be done, he's got himself into this position in the first place because he has far more power here in Cottonwood than anyone else does. He's a rich man, you know. And people with money tend to get what they want. Last time I stood up to him, a bunch of my gates got left open. He was in the clear because he was out of the village at the time, who knows where. Not to say he didn't slip someone a few quid to do it, but stuff like that causes problems. A cow is worth several hundred pounds to me, and if one wanders out in front of a car, it's my insurance that's paying out. Inviting more misfortune on myself isn't a risk I want to take.'

'Alan—'

'No.' Alan shook his head. For the first time Emily sensed a simmering of anger beneath the calm surface of his face. 'If you want to go riling up the village's most powerful man, that's fine, but don't forget you don't live round here. You get to walk away whenever you choose. You don't have to deal with it.'

'Can I show you something?'

Alan sighed. 'Sure. What?'

Emily's jacket was hanging from a hook in the hall. While Alan waited in the kitchen, she went to retrieve it, pulling the letter out of the inside pocket. She handed it to Alan, who frowned as he turned it over in his hands.

'Where did you get this?' he asked.

'Would you believe me if I said Germany? Out of a hollow in an old oak tree?'

Alan looked up. 'This writing … may I open it?'

'Of course. This is why I came to Cottonwood. Sure, things haven't gone as I'd expected, but that letter is the real reason why I'm here.'

Alan slipped the sheet of paper out of the envelope and read it. Still frowning, he reached up and wiped a tear from the corner of his eye.

'You recognise the handwriting, don't you?'

Alan nodded. He looked down at a notebook lying open on the table. Emily had seen it as soon as she had come in, reading enough of it to be sure. The composition half-finished on the left-hand page was titled "*My Weekend Diary by John Rowe*".

'The lad was calling for help,' Alan said. 'How he found about this tree, I have no idea.'

'A school project, perhaps? He probably read about it on the internet. It's a unique way to ask, that's for sure.'

Alan sighed and shook his head. Emily felt an

overwhelming urge to give him a hug, but resisted. After a moment, Alan looked up at her and smiled. 'Imagine sending a letter to a tree? He didn't even ask his own father about it. What kind of person have I been to ignore the needs of my own son?'

'It's not your fault,' Emily said. 'But it's about time things changed. The feudal lord in his castle isn't just ruining Christmas for you and me. He's ruining it for the kids. Sure, I don't live around here, and it's not really any of my business, but are you really going to let him get away with it?'

22

WATER ISSUES

'To what do I owe this pleasure?' Karen said. 'Are you drinking wine?'

Emily smiled. 'I'm on my second glass.'

'Good. I could do with a natter. David and his family are watching *Polar Express* for the nineteenth time, so you've given me a good excuse to sneak out to the kitchen and slug a couple of glasses of expensive port. How's it going down there?'

'I'm about to start a revolution.'

'Huh. Going all Che Guevara on me are you?'

'Perhaps not that intense. I've decided that Cottonwood will go to the Christmas Ball, one way or another. Moody hot Scrooges be damned.'

'Wow, that must be exciting. A bit more than getting drunk and fat and watching Christmas telly.'

'I thought you liked it over at David's? You can come down and be my chief of staff if you like. I'll need someone to drive the bulldozer when we block the tyrant's driveway.'

'Sounds like fun. Where on earth did you find a bulldozer?'

'It's just a rough idea. That or trapping him with a mile of tinsel tied around the outside of his house.'

'You're a devil. No stocking presents for you, I imagine.'

'I'll take the trade.'

They turned to more trivial matters for a while before Karen made her excuses and they said goodnight. Emily curled up on the sofa with a third glass of wine, reading a Stephen King while the fire crackled in the hearth and a CD of Christmas songs performed by a classical orchestra played quietly in the background. On the coffee table lay a list Alan had given her, twenty-five names and addresses of local people who would most likely join their resistance against Trower and his Christmas-avoidance. She had tried drafting a note explaining her cause, but figured it would be far easier just to get up early and do some door-knocking. That had been another of Elaine's philosophies: that the best persuasion was done face to face. Emily had spent many a long afternoon wandering around local villages knocking on doors and handing out discount coupons. With the exception of the hillier places it had been a pleasant enough experience, and the relentless custom Elaine's teahouse had experienced was testament to her theory's worth.

It was just after ten o'clock. Exhausted, Emily swallowed the last of her wine and prepared to go up to bed. She had one foot on the bottom stair when a knock came on the door.

Who could be visiting at this time of night? Emily felt a little spooked, and considered just ignoring the visitor. However, the person would see her lights were still on.

'Who is it?' she asked.

'It's me. Nathan.'

Of course. The most socially awkward person she had met in Cottonwood so far. Who else would show up at such an inappropriate time of night?'

'What do you want?'

'Can I come in?'

Emily had a sudden pang of realisation that she hadn't yet turned off the lights of her Christmas tree. Nor would the solar lights in the garden—which usually lasted until around midnight—have gone out yet. He might be the owner of the property, but as a tenant she had rights. Just in case, she pulled up the local police's phone number and had it ready in case he caused trouble.

She opened the door.

Nathan stood there, tall and imposing. Snowflakes flecked his dark hair and slowly melted into the fabric on his jacket's shoulders. Before even looking at Emily, he peered past her into the hall, his eyes fearful of what horrific image of Christmas he might see.

'Are you all right?' she asked.

He looked at her, eyes focusing. 'I … ah, came to say I was sorry about earlier today. I'm afraid I don't have many visitors, and certain … things … upset me a little. I hope I wasn't too … demonic.'

The submission in his voice allowed Emily to take the upper hand. 'You certainly don't know how to appreciate people's efforts,' she said. Then, with a smile, she added, 'But it's Christmas, so I'll forgive you.'

'Yes, it's Christmas,' Nathan echoed, again looking elsewhere.

'I gave your cake to someone else,' Emily said, as though the knowledge of what he'd lost out of might drive a knife of guilt into his heart.

'That's good,' he said. 'I'm not much of a cake person.'

Emily shrugged. Nathan stood awkwardly for a moment, still peering into the hall. The seconds ticked past without either speaking. Nathan, as always, was remarkably easy on the eye, but Emily felt invisible as the walls and skirting boards took up all of his attention.

'Was there something else?' she said at last. 'I was about to go to bed.'

Nathan looked at her. 'Yes, actually. The reason I called … the council contacted me earlier. They've detected a leaking water pipe and need to do some excavations to locate it.'

'Oh? Where?'

'In the plot to the rear of this property. The back garden. They'll be here at nine a.m. tomorrow. I'm afraid you'll need to remove all your … decorations in order for them to get to the garden.'

Emily stared at him. Was this another deliberate ploy to stop her celebrating Christmas? Not to mention how would he even know about the illuminations in the garden unless he'd been in the house or been spying on her?

Right now, though, she was too tired to argue.

'Okay, fine. I'll do it in the morning.'

'Thank you. They'll appreciate your assistance. Just to be warned, they'll be noisy and it might take a few days, they said. If you wished to leave early I would be prepared to refund your entire stay.'

There was the crux of it. He wanted her gone.

Emily shook her head. 'It's fine,' she said, meeting his stare and holding it. 'I'm having far too much of a good time here in Cottonwood. I'm sure a little noise won't bother me.'

Nathan lifted an eyebrow. Even after everything, part of Emily didn't want him to leave.

'Well, okay then. I just thought I should warn you.'

With that, he let himself out.

After he was gone, Emily stared at the closed door, slowly shaking her head.

23

GENERATORS

Never one to sleep late due to getting the teahouse ready for opening, Emily bounced out of bed—with only a moderate wine hangover—at just after six o'clock. With coffee in hand she set about moving her illuminations to the sides of the garden for the council workmen to get at the lawn. She refused to take them down completely as Nathan had requested, because part of her didn't expect the council to actually show up.

With the job done, a second coffee drunk and some cornflakes eaten, Emily headed across the road to the shop.

Peter was just opening up, carrying signs and a rack of newspapers outside. Emily greeted him and he gave her a warm if slightly reluctant smile.

'I brought you something,' she said, holding out a Tupperware box.

'What's this?'

'Eccles cakes.'

Peter's eyes lit up. 'Thanks.'

'Don't eat them all at once. In exchange, do you think you could do a favour for me?'

Peter gave a brief chuckle. 'Depends what it is.'

'I need to print a document and make a few photocopies.' She pointed at the post office sign. 'Any chance?'

'I'll check with Mum, but I'm sure it won't be a problem. What's it about?'

'Christmas.'

Peter gave a slow nod. 'Oh. Well, I suppose you'd better come inside.'

Emily followed him into the shop. While it would have been easy to drive back to the teahouse and use Elaine's old desktop and printer, Emily was keen to involve the locals where she could. It helped sew them into the lining of her plan, make them feel they were truly part of it.

A few minutes later, having found Kelly setting up inside the shop, Emily held up a wad of photocopies, then picked one off the top and handed it over.

'Thanks,' she said. 'And here's your copy.'

'*Reinstatement of the Cottonwood Christmas Carnival*,' Kelly read. '*An invitation to a planning meeting to be held in the Smuggler's Bar at the Inn on the Green at 4 p.m. on Thursday December 19th*.' She looked up at Emily. 'You really think you can pull this off? You're cutting it awful fine.'

'That's why we can't waste any time.'

'Have you got anyone in on this yet?'

'Skip over at the pub, and Alan Rowe,' Emily said.

Kelly sighed. 'Well, if we're going to sink the ship,

we might as well all drown together. Peter and I will be there.'

Emily smiled. 'Fantastic. Right, I'd better get on the road with these. I have construction guys coming in half an hour.'

'Construction?'

'The council wants to dig up my back lawn to look for a leaking water pipe.'

Kelly rolled her eyes. 'See? What did I tell you? Trower, he's like a disease. You have no idea what you're getting yourself into.'

Emily headed out. She wanted to be present when the council showed up, and she only had a few minutes. Luckily the central part of the village was cramped close together. Using Alan's address list, she knocked on a handful of doors around the square, handing over flyers and explaining who she was and her plan.

The response was overwhelmingly positive. A couple of people told her they'd show up at three just to get front row seats. At another house, Emily talked to a wife leaning around a father adjusting a tie in a hall mirror while two young children hung onto her arm. When the father announced he would get off work early for the meeting, the two children cheered.

Nathaniel Trower's empire of oppression was about to be toppled.

She got back to her holiday let just in time to greet the council workers. An overweight, balding man in a luminous yellow jacket introduced himself as Jack and promised to deal with the problem as soon as possible. Together with two younger subordinates, Graham and Leon, they set to work carrying their tools through the house to the back garden.

As soon as the council workers were set up, Emily gave them a key so they could get in and out, then set out again on her own mission, taking with her a bag of cooking gear for her planned meeting with Veronica.

By the time she got to the café at about midday, she was exhausted from traipsing around the village. She had visited all the addresses on Alan's list except for a couple of outlying properties she would drive to later. Without exception, people had been delighted to speak to her. Everyone free to attend the meeting told her they would be there, except for one old lady who used a walker to get around, and told Emily, 'I'll be there in spirit, but hopefully not all of it just yet. You bring that tyrant to his knees for me.'

In Veronica's café, she slumped into a chair. 'I'll have today's special,' she said.

'Coffee?'

Emily laughed. 'Sure. Whatever you're making.'

Veronica beamed. 'Today's special is coffee.'

'You might want to make the daily special a little more exotic, but it's a good start.'

'What, like coffee with honey in it?'

'There you go.'

Veronica grabbed a chalkboard off the counter and began scribbling on it. 'Coffee with honey in it is today's special,' she said, propping the board back up.

'We'll have to work on your phrasing, but that's more like it,' Emily said. 'I see you've removed the drapes off the windows.'

'So people can see in, and customers can see out,' Veronica said. 'Like you were telling me.'

'You're getting the hang of this, I think.'

'Thanks.'

Veronica brought over the coffee. She set it down in front of Emily, gave a polite curtsey and asked if Emily wanted anything else, then returned to the counter and came back with a coffee of her own. She slumped down opposite Emily, her professionalism forgotten.

'Off duty now?'

'Yep.'

Emily passed across one of her remaining photocopies. 'This is the plan,' she said.

'You're really going to take him on?'

'Why not?' Emily smiled. 'It's Christmas. Time to spread some cheer.' She tapped a line near the bottom. 'Can you arrange some kind of coffee stand?'

'What does that entail?'

'We're going to hold the carnival over Sunday and Monday. Yes, that's in three days, and yes, I know that sounds impossible. I have some contacts, however, and if everyone pulls together, we can make it happen.'

'How can people get organised for a big event in two days?'

'The longer we spend preparing, the more time Trower will have for his sabotage operation,' Emily said. 'This way we can get it happening before he has a chance to do anything about it.'

'Where are you planning to hold it?'

'In the village hall car park. There's plenty of room.'

Veronica whistled through her teeth. 'Cottonwood Parish Council will never allow it.'

Emily shook her head. 'There is no parish council. Only Trower. It's all a con and the whole village fell for it.'

'What?'

Emily briefly explained what she had discovered. Veronica just shook her head.

'He has a real chip on his shoulder, doesn't he?'

'It has to be seen to be believed.'

'I wonder why?'

∽

After their coffees, Emily showed Veronica a couple of recipes while they ate some sandwiches Veronica had prepared. Emily wanted to stay longer, but there were a million things she had to organise before the meeting, so she headed back to her holiday let.

The council workmen were sitting in their van eating pasties and drinking coffee out of flasks. Emily noticed to her amusement that they were all wearing Christmas hats, so she knocked on the door until Jack wound down the window.

'Did you fix it?' she asked.

'Not yet. Pretty cold out, and the ground's a bit frozen. I'm sure it won't be long.'

'Why don't you come inside and eat in the kitchen? It can't be pleasant sitting in there.'

'Not the most comfortable,' Jack said. 'Graham had eggs for breakfast.'

'Only the one,' Graham said from the back. 'It must have upset me a little bit.'

Smiling, Emily waved them after her, then went into the kitchen and put a few mince pies in the oven to warm. A few minutes later she had rustled up some eggnog and was serving it to the three eager workmen sitting around the kitchen counter.

'Have you found what you're after?' she said, as they tucked hungrily into mince pies topped with clotted cream.

'Not yet,' Jack said. 'To be honest, we're not sure what we're looking for, only that we'll know it when we see it.'

'What exactly are you looking for?'

'We were told there might be a leak under your lawn.'

'What kind of leak?'

'No idea. We've checked your water and gas and there's no sign of anything, but we were told to dig, so we dig.'

Emily looked out into the back garden. A trench a metre wide and three long was slowly collecting flecks of snow as the heavy clouds overhead began to disgorge. The rest of the garden was a mess of boot prints in snow and discarded ornaments. However, despite having to pass through the house to get gear from their van, the floor was spotless.

'Is that a pneumatic drill?' she asked, pointing at something leaning against a fence.

'It is indeed,' Jack said. 'In case we hit rock.'

'And it's powered by a generator?'

'That's right. We always bring our own power source, never use the customer's.'

Emily rubbed her nose. 'Do you think you could make this job last until next Tuesday?'

'The twenty-third?'

'Well, night of the twenty-second.'

Jack shrugged. 'If you really want us around that long.'

'See, the thing is, it's Christmas, and I'm planning a little event. I'm pretty sure you're digging for no reason, but if it's okay I'd really like to borrow that generator. And do you think you could borrow a couple more?'

'Three smaller ones in the van,' Leon said.

'And do you have a ladder by any chance?'

Jack smiled as he finished off a mince pie. 'Miss, what exactly are you getting us into?'

'You don't need to worry,' Emily said. 'Just know that there will be a lot more mince pies where those came from.'

'Then count us in,' Jack said, as Graham and Leon nodded in agreement. 'No fun digging trenches in the snow anyway.'

24

MEETING

AFTER THE WORKMEN GOT BACK TO THEIR PSEUDO-digging, which, via Emily's instructions, now included 'as many coffee and mince pie breaks as you can handle,' Emily found herself with an hour to spare before the meeting started.

Needing a break, she retrieved her laptop and went online, at first putting in place a few things for the upcoming carnival including an advertising spot reserved in tomorrow's local paper—which she could cancel if the group decided the carnival was too big a risk—and a couple of emails to old contacts of her grandmother's. One was a company which specialised in industrial-sized tents used for wedding parties and fetes, another a company which provided PA systems.

Emails sent, she still had half an hour before she had to go, so had an idle around on social media to unwind a little. Browsing Facebook, she wondered on the off chance if Trower was on there. It wasn't a common name, so she doubted she would be presented with a long list to trawl through. The search function, however, came up with nothing, but there was a Liselle Trower listed who lived in Brighton. Nathan's sister? It couldn't possibly be, but Emily sent her a private message just in case.

Liselle happened to be online, and sent her an almost immediate message back. Yes, she was Nathan's sister. Emily gave her a brief explanation of who she was before asking if she could perhaps call Liselle for a chat. Liselle agreed. To Emily's complete surprise, a minute later a woman's face appeared on screen via Skype. Like Nathan, she was hopelessly attractive, but when she smiled it had far more of the sun in it than his ever did.

'Very nice to meet you, Emily,' Liselle said. 'I have to say, this is rather unexpected. You said you've met my brother? That must have been a delightful experience.' Liselle laughed. 'What would you like to know?'

~

The front bar of the pub was empty besides Skip, who was polishing a glass when Emily came in, five minutes late.

'There you are,' he said. 'Quick, get back there before there's a riot.'

'Did many people show up?'

'All of them,' Skip said. 'I don't know who you are or what power you have over people, but you've got them practically frothing at the mouth. In some cases literally. I, um, felt it appropriate to offer a free round of hot chocolates.'

'With marshmallows?'

'Of course. Hence the frothing.'

Emily headed for the Smuggler's Bar. It was down a short corridor and she could hear a rumble of incoherent voices as she hurried down it to the door at the far end. Taking a deep breath, she pushed through, and found herself faced with around fifty people sitting on wooden chairs pilfered from the bar's rarely used restaurant. There, near the front, was Alan, who gave her a reassuring smile. Beside him sat his children, Lily who gave Emily a thumbs-up, and John a shy smile. Next to them were Kelly and Peter, who was making surreptitious glances across at Veronica, who was sitting by the wall, and making surreptitious glances back at him. A couple of rows back sat Mrs. Taylor, while a couple of places across from her was Barney from Royston's Lumber Yard, who must have heard about the meeting from a friend. Of the rest, she recognised most from her house calls, but there were at least a dozen others she had never seen before.

She had started the ball rolling, and word of mouth had done the rest.

'Hello, everyone,' she said, as a hush fell over the group. 'Thank you so much for coming. I recognise a few of you, but it's good to see some other faces too. Welcome.'

A small round of applause spread across the crowd. Near the back, someone she didn't recognise called, 'And who exactly are you, young lady?'

'That's a good question,' Emily said. 'Until now I wasn't quite sure. You see, I only came here by chance. On October the first this year, my grandmother died. However, she wasn't just my grandmother, but also my grandfather, and more than that, my mother and father and brothers and sisters all rolled into one. You see, my parents died when I was very young, and I had no siblings. My grandmother raised me from the age of three. And frankly, she did a really good job. To say she was my world is an understatement. I couldn't have understood the void her death would leave until it happened.'

She paused for breath, realising she was crying. Murmurs spread across the crowd. She noticed Veronica and a couple of others staring at her, mouths agape.

'My grandmother, Elaine Wilson, was a remarkable woman. Not only was she the light and soul of our community, but she ran its most successful business and always seemed to know what would make people happy. I lived in her shadow and I was happy there, but when she died, it was like the sun was shining in my eyes for the first time and I didn't know what to do. I didn't know where to hide.'

More murmurs. A couple of sniffs came from somewhere in the audience. Someone blew their nose.

'I couldn't handle the pressure. Not only was I grieving for her loss, but I was expected to step up into her position and take over her business. You see, she left everything to me, and her will requested that I continue the business in her memory.' Emily took a deep breath. 'So what did I do?'

Everyone was staring at her, their faces rapt, their eyes unblinking. Emily swallowed, aware her hands were shaking.

'I shut the doors. I locked myself away and I hid from the world. I could barely bring myself to leave the house until a good friend showed up one day and told me to pull myself together. I couldn't face opening up the business again, so instead of hiding, I started running away. We went travelling across Europe, and honestly, if she hadn't needed to go back to work and the fear of being alone not been too great, I would have carried on running away forever. However, during the trip—on the last day, actually—I came across a letter. A letter from someone in this village, crying out for help.'

At this John Rowe's head snapped up. Emily met his gaze and smiled, even though she had already decided not to embarrass him by naming him outright.

'This letter was asking for Christmas to return to Cottonwood. The idea of a village without a Christmas horrified me, as Christmas had been my grandmother's favourite time of year, when she had insisted above everything else that we make people as happy as possible. Her café became a communal living room, welcoming to everyone, full of laughter, singing, and really good food. It was a spirit I could never forget, and it was with that memory that I came here, running away from my own responsibilities, wondering if in Cottonwood I might find out something about myself.'

She paused again, aware she had been running away with herself, her heart beating, her words starting to lose their shape. Speeches had always been Elaine's thing, with Emily standing patiently at her grandmother's side, waiting to be given the all clear to spring into action. Now, with her grandmother gone, it was time to step up into the spotlight.

'I might not have my grandmother's gift for creating happiness, but when I came here and found that Christmas had been squeezed out of this village, I got this crazy idea in my head that I, a complete stranger to most of you, could do something to bring it back. However, I'm just one person, and one person on their own has no power to do anything. We all have to step up, put a hand in the air and shout together, "I want Christmas back!"'

As she shouted, she realised no one else had shouted with her. Her voice cracked, with "back" ending with a chalkboard nails shriek. Sweat rolled down her face as she glanced at the crowd, and saw stunned faces slowly turn to smiles. The first clap came from Veronica, who was holding a corner of her dress over her nose. Slowly the applause spread, until people started to rise to their feet. Emily stared as the whole crowd stood and cheered for her.

'One, two, three!' Alan shouted.

'We want Christmas back!' shouted everyone together, although two grinning boys near the front shouted, 'Our maths teacher's a pig,' at the same time, hoping no one would hear. For their efforts they received a stern glare from a wiry lady sat on the other side of the room.

As the applause died down and people returned to their seats, Emily pulled a sheet of paper from her pocket.

'Thank you so much,' she said. 'Now, I think it's best to have a long talk about what we can achieve.' She held up her piece of paper. 'I have a few ideas for an itinerary. I wrote them in pencil because I couldn't find a pen.'

25

KRAMPUS

Emily was sitting outside the pub with a glass of wine, watching the snow gently fall over the village green when Alan Rowe appeared beside her.

'This seat free?' he asked, pulling out a chair beside her, then waiting for a few polite seconds until she smiled and told him to sit down. Above them, the snow pattered gently on the parasols Skip had erected on the pavement in front of the pub, sheltering a dozen tired planners from the falling snow. Behind her, a large paraffin heater provided warmth to the back of Emily's legs, a blanket to the front. A couple of dozen other people were still inside the pub, making a day of it, but Emily was exhausted. She hadn't realised how much being a leader would take out of her.

'You've done a brilliant job,' Alan said. 'I think people are hoping you'll come and live here in Cottonwood.'

She smiled. 'It's a pleasant enough place. Perhaps

I'll get a summer house. You can show me a few of the local footpaths.'

'It would be my pleasure.' He held her gaze for a few seconds before looking away. Emily thought she saw a hint of a blush beneath the upper part of his beard, but it could easily have been the pint he was halfway through.

'Seriously,' he said, taking a moment before he looked back at her, 'it's like you've woken the village up. It used to be like this, you know. Always a friendly face in the pub or sitting over on the green. Then, we all went to sleep….'

'I'm happy to have made a difference. It'll take a lot of hard work to pull it all off, though.'

'It was a stroke of genius doing it as a charity event.'

'It makes it harder for Trower to shut down. Particularly as the county council has granted permission.'

'How did you pull that off?'

'Trower's not the only one with friends on the council. Although, to be fair, I'm trading off my grandmother's favours. She did more for our community than anyone. She funded a refurbishment of the public toilets, donated a patch of land to be made into a community space, and was the chairperson for our local parish council. She supervised local litter-picking events, organised the neighbourhood watch, arranged free daycare for low-income families with children … honestly, when I look back now, I wonder when she slept.'

'And she taught you how to organise things?'

Emily shook her head. 'I didn't realise it at the time, but I suppose she must have done. Mostly, she would leave me in charge of the teahouse while she was off doing community events. I never felt in charge, but now that she's gone … it feels natural. She taught me by letting me learn by myself.'

'The best way,' Alan said. 'I wish I could organise things the way you do.'

Emily smiled. 'I think you do all right. You run a farm while raising two wonderful children. It must have been hard, you know, after your wife….'

Alan nodded. 'There were days I couldn't go on,' he said quietly. 'But then I looked at their faces and I went on. Because you have to, don't you?'

Emily nodded. 'That's right.'

'But let's not be too morose, shall we? You have to think forward, and our forward is creating a wonderful Christmas carnival.'

Emily laughed. 'That will also pay for a refurbishment of the village hall. Are you clear on what you need to do tomorrow?'

Alan held up his fingers. 'Help the council lads clear that big pine on the edge of the car park of weeds and give it a trim. Then, get some ladders up and get it decorated.'

'Perfect. That's our tree sorted.'

'Then get the snowplow out and clear the roads, making sure to leave a big pile in front of a certain party pooper's drive.'

'Good job.'

'He'll still be able to get out, though. We can't lock him up. What are we going to do if he starts on one of his sabotage missions? I mean, despite causing a bit of trouble and costing a bit of money, it's mostly been harmless, but what if he ramps it up a level?'

'I'm going to talk to him tomorrow,' Emily said, remembering her conversation from this afternoon with Liselle. 'I'm sure by now he'll want to kick me out, but that won't make any difference. I've had five people just this afternoon offer me a place to stay if he does.'

'Make that six,' Alan said. 'We have a ton of space. Before Katherine died, we also ran a B&B. However, Lily might wear you out.'

'She's a great kid,' Emily said. The idea of moving in with a family as warm and welcoming as the Rowe's made her feel ... she smiled and shook her head. 'They're both great kids,' she added, her words falling over themselves a little too quickly. 'When ey're old enough for summer jobs, send them my way.'

Alan gave her an awkward smile. 'So ... you're going to open up the teahouse again, are you?'

Emily frowned. She hadn't thought about it, but the words had popped out as though there could be no other option.

'I'm still thinking about it,' she said. 'Maybe.'

Alan looked down at his fingers for a moment before looking up. 'I, um, don't think anyone would mind if you decided to open another one right here in Cottonwood. The kids and me ... we'd be there on opening day.'

~

She kept it to just one glass of wine before bidding goodnight to Alan and whoever was left in the pub. She stumbled back to her holiday let, got a fire going, and then lay on the sofa for a while, thinking over the day's events. The villagers had totally rallied around her, and plans for the Christmas carnival were flying ahead at full speed. It was set to be an epic event, but there was an underlying concern which wouldn't go away.

Nathan.

She knew she had to confront him again, because it was impossible that he wouldn't find out about the carnival. Like a dictator thrown from power, he wouldn't go easily into the night, but this wasn't war, this was Christmas. She didn't want him exiled, barricaded into his house by a mound of snow. He might have deprived the village of Christmas for the past two years, but if ever there was a season for forgiveness and reintegration, this was it.

Whether he was interested was another matter.

She waited until the fire had died down, then went back into the kitchen and washed up her glass. Before going up to bed, she went out into the garden and stood for a couple of minutes, listening carefully. At first, all she heard was the gentle pattering of the snow, now nearly ten centimetres deep, but finally, over the top, she heard it: the whine of a quadcopter's propellers.

The drone was up there somewhere, watching over the village. Nathan, perhaps gleefully sat at a computer screen and searching for lights in the night, was watching. The sound increased as the drone came closer, and Emily got the distinct impression it was hanging in the sky right overhead, its camera looking down at her garden.

Uprooted by the unnecessary excavations, the lights were out. Tonight, Nathan would be satisfied. But tomorrow … preparations for the Christmas carnival began in earnest. He would surely know. The snow was about to hit the fan in a big way, and Emily felt a tickle of nerves, wondering how he would react.

After a two-year absence, Christmas was returning to Cottonwood. Emily's biggest fear, though, was that Krampus would also show up to ruin it.

26

PREPARATIONS

Emily crawled out of bed to the sound of knocking. Throwing a dressing gown around her shoulders, she staggered downstairs, aware it was still dark outside. The knocking continued at a frenzied pace until Emily called out, 'All right, I'm coming!'

Steeling herself for an argument with Nathan, who had perhaps come to tell her that the roof needed immediate replacement, or her hallway was required to store a crane, or even that he had decided overnight to level the three holiday lets and erect a block of flats in their place and that a wrecking ball was waiting right outside … she was somewhat surprised to find Veronica standing on her doorstep, holding two overflowing supermarket bags in her hands.

'What time do you call this?' Emily asked, wondering if she'd drunk more wine than she realised, or whether she was just exhausted.

'Six,' Veronica said. 'Just like you told me. I got the stuff. Come on, let me in. It's freezing out here.'

As Emily stepped back to let Veronica in, she frowned. 'What stuff?'

'The cooking stuff. You said we need to make ten chocolate logs for the cake stand.'

'Oh, right.'

'Starting at six. It says it on your schedule.'

'The one I wrote in pencil?'

Veronica shrugged. 'Yeah. I mean, you wrote seven, but I thought we need to get started so I rubbed it out and wrote six.'

'Oh, right.'

'You don't mind?'

'Well, no. It was very … productive of you.'

Veronica beamed. 'Thanks. God, it's colder in here than it is outside. Why don't you put the heating on?'

Emily gave a tired nod. 'Sure.' She didn't yet feel awake enough to notice.

'Are you ready to get started?'

Emily nodded again. 'I might take a quick shower first.'

'No probs. I'll get started on the log mix. Mind if I put these down? They weigh a ton.'

Emily shook her head.

'Thanks. Oh, and I got this.' Veronica reached into one of the bags and pulled out a Christmas hat, which she perched on top of the knitting needles sticking out of the top of her hair. Emily wondered absently how Veronica managed to get up early enough to set her hair into such an intricate tower of delight. Then, as Veronica gave an extravagant yawn, Emily realised the girl had probably been up all night.

'Might take a nap in a bit, if that's okay,' Veronica said.

Emily nodded. 'You and me both.'

∽

Two hours later, with the ten chocolate logs in varied stages of construction, Veronica was snoozing on the sofa while Emily made some phone calls in the kitchen. Everything was going well. The snow was threatening to derail everything, of course, but Alan had got his plow working and had managed to clear a way through to the duel carriageway exit a couple of miles distant, where, by some miracle, the snow had all melted off. Cottonwood, it appeared, was situated in a bit of a microclimate cold pocket, but that could work to their advantage.

With the roads in one direction cleared, and Garry Timpson, owner of Fingles, the farm adjacent to Rowe Farm, providing a free shuttle service in the back of his Land Rover up to the bus stop by the duel carriageway, people were able to get in without having to drive through the danger end of the village. It was still early, of course, but so far there had been no sign of Nathan Trower.

Not that Emily intended to keep their rebellion a secret. Sooner or later all would be revealed, but she hoped not until the snowball of goodwill had reached an unstoppable stage. And with only a couple of stalls currently onsite, they weren't quite at that stage just yet.

Elaine's contacts had come good. Several local food stall services had been bookable even at such a late date, as had a mobile disco-karaoke company. Planning the carnival to go over Sunday-Monday had proved a stroke of genius, because several services busy on Saturday were freed up on the adjacent days. Emily had even managed book a Christmas songs covers band called Sweet Slade Crosby for the Monday night. Veronica, too, had made a call, and had a "mate" who was apparently a "magician" and would be happy to do a free hour show in exchange for a few beers and a picture in the local paper.

The council had also come up trumps, not only granting permission to hold the event but allowing an alcohol sales license for the two days, and a noise curfew of midnight.

All without the head of the invisible parish council finding out.

'So it's going well?' Karen asked.

Emily, who hadn't been able to resist a quick personal call in the midst of the maelstrom of business, nodded. 'So far, so good. The locals have been fantastic. You can tell they really wanted their Christmas back, and they've thrown themselves into it.'

'They needed a catalyst. You must be very proud.'

Emily shook her head. 'I didn't do much really. I just gave them a nudge in the right direction.'

'Come on, I know you better than that. Are you starting to realise yet?'

'Realise what?'

'That you can exist out of your grandmother's shadow. That, despite what you always say, you're capable of doing whatever you want.'

'I wouldn't go that far. It has been a good distraction, though. It's been nice to have something to take my mind off everything else.'

'Well, I'm pleased for you. I can't wait to see what you've achieved.'

'You'll come down?'

'David and his dad are out putting the chains on the mini-bus as we speak. We're bringing the whole clan down.'

'That'll be great.'

'Will it? You'd better have plenty of food. They're like locusts, eating their way through everything.'

'I'll be prepared.'

'Great.' Karen sighed. 'Oh no, bad news. The future M-I-L just got the Twister out. Looks like I've got to go.'

They both hung up. After a hot morning in the kitchen, Emily fancied a walk, so she checked in on Veronica, informing the dozing girl of her decision and receiving a grunt in response, before heading out into the snow.

It had been snowing steadily all night and was now fifteen centimetres deep in places. Emily was unable to hide a squee feeling at the sight of it, having grown up in Birchtide, which never seemed to get much snow even if it was dumping in neighbouring villages. As she headed up the road in the direction of the village hall she passed Alan on his tractor with the plow shovel attached and gave him a wave. Alan had cleared the centre of the roads, but the snow had to go somewhere, so great mounds now lined the streets, much to the delight of several groups of children who were out battering each other with snowballs or building immense, wonky snowmen. With a wry smile, Emily wondered if there was a rule against that, too.

Passing Veronica's place, she saw what had apparently kept the girl up all night—a delightful pattern of fairy lights had been hung from garden trellises to spell out *Merry Christmas Everyone*. In a moment of red-cheeked coyness, Veronica had confessed that Peter, out walking Rudolph, had offered to help, so she had stretched it out as long as possible, before the pair of them had retired to a table in front of her coffee machine 'to talk about books and stuff.' By the time they were done, there 'weren't no point going to bed then, was there?', to which Emily had just laughed and told Veronica to go and take a nap.

Currently switched off, the lights would look beautiful later when they came on, as would those of several other properties, the defiance of Trower's laws apparently having a liberating effect on several locals. Emily just hoped it didn't all come back to slap her in the face. However, she did have a contingency plan up her sleeve, and she was anticipating her next meeting with Trower with great excitement.

Up in the village hall's car park, several local men were erecting a wooden gate across the entrance with "Christmas Carnival" written over the top. Others were clearing away the snow, or hanging fairy lights over the front of the hall. The huge pine to the left of the entrance had been cleared of vines and creepers, and a couple of ladders lay on the ground nearby. Just as she arrived, the council van pulled in, and Jack wound down a window.

'Morning,' he said. 'Looking good up here.'

'Thanks for coming,' Emily said.

'Got the gear in the van,' Jack said. 'We're going to unload up here, where me and Graham will take care of the tree and the generators. Leon's going to go park down outside yours, give the impression we're hard at work if that mate of yours shows up.'

'Sounds perfect.'

Jack gave her a thumbs-up, then bumped the van carefully through the snow and parked in a corner. Emily headed inside to see what was going on.

Beside the stage at one end of the village hall, Mrs. Taylor was directing a group of other older people loaded down with tinsel, paper chains, and fairy lights. A small plastic tree stood in one corner, surrounded by fake Christmas presents. A couple of local kids were wiping the dust off with towels, while a couple more sat in a corner, wrapping other generic cardboard boxes with colourful paper.

'Looks brilliant,' Emily said to the towering Mrs. Taylor, who was giraffe-like as she leaned over from the stage above. 'You've done a great job.'

Mrs. Taylor took a deep breath and smiled. 'It's so liberating,' she said. 'I can feel Christmas in the air again at long last. What a wonderful event this is going to be.' Her smile dropped. 'Have you had any trouble yet from yours truly? He's been notable by his absence.'

Emily shook her head. 'Not yet. I'm going to visit him later. I don't think there's any point in this being a secret.'

'If you want some moral support, just ask. We can follow you with a full phalanx of pitchforks if necessary.'

Emily laughed. 'I don't think that will be necessary. This was my idea though, so I should be the one who visits him.'

'As you wish. And don't forget to give him my card.'

Emily patted the pocket of her jacket. After a private discussion following the end of the meeting, Mrs. Taylor had given her a business card. 'I'm officially retired, but I'd be prepared to make an exception,' she had told Emily.

Emily shook her head. 'I won't forget,' she said.

'I hope it goes well.'

'Me too.'

Emily thanked Mrs. Taylor again, then headed back outside. She was on her way back to the holiday let when a man came bustling up through the snow. He wore a leather jacket and carried a motorcycle helmet under one arm.

'Ms. Wilson?' he asked. 'I've heard you're in charge.'

'Yes, that's me.'

The man stuck out a hand. 'Ted Billingham. Reverend, Cottonwood Parish Church. I hear you're reincarnating the Christmas carnival.'

'Um, yes. You're the local reverend? You, um—'

'Don't look much like a priest?' Billingham laughed. 'Nope. In these conditions I don't look much like a biker either. Looks can be deceiving and all that. In lieu of all these goings on, I was wondering if you wouldn't mind a church service done on the Sunday morning. Plus, do you think you've got a spot on the itinerary for the local caroler group?'

'Oh, that would be great. I wasn't even aware there was one.'

Billingham rolled his eyes. 'That tyrant Saul slapped us with a noise restriction notice, but like good Philistines we've continued to practice in secret. Well, not quite, but in Fitton, just across the valley there. We'd be delighted to make a triumphant return now the walls of Jericho appear to have fallen.'

'That would be just great. I'll pencil you into the schedule. Thanks.'

'Nice. Right, off to take advantage of these conditions and do some terrifically dangerous turns in the snow. Godspeed, young lady.'

He gave Emily a military salute before rushing off to a powerful Honda road bike leaning nearby, its shiny chassis spotted with snow.

'You've met the vicar, then?' came a voice to Emily's left, and she turned to find Kelly Chambers beside her, a plastic snow shovel in hand, a bobble hat pulled down over her head.

'Interesting chap,' Emily said.

'He used to be a local heartthrob,' Kelly said with a smile. 'In his youth he rode in motorcycle grand prix and even presented a cable television show about motorbikes before abruptly finding God. Until Trower shut down most of the church services for ridiculous arbitrary reasons, Cottonwood was probably the only parish in the country where church attendance was on the rise.'

Emily smiled. 'I would probably go if I lived here.'

'He certainly makes it interesting. Anyway, how is everything going?'

'Good, by the look of things.'

'No sign of the Dark Lord yet?'

Emily winced. 'Not yet.'

'He won't let this go, you know that, don't you? If you want some moral support—'

Emily lifted a hand. 'Pitchforks at the ready, right?'

'You've got it.'

Kelly wished Emily well and headed off to her snow clearing duty. Emily glanced at her watch, finding it was still not yet ten o'clock. It was probably best to get her confrontation with Nathan out of the way.

'Right, Emily,' she said to herself with a determined grimace. 'Time to put your head back into the lion's mouth.'

27

FAMILY VALUES

Nathan Trower's house looked as unlived in as it had before, the only difference now being that the driveway was ankle-deep with snow. Emily paused at the end of the driveway, observing a line of boot prints that led up to the front door. Alan hadn't plowed this section of road, and a line of tyre tracks were clearly visible coming up from the valley and stopping outside Nathan's house, where they reversed and then headed back the way they had come.

A home delivery. From the way the tracks had begun to fill up again, Emily guessed it had been a couple of hours ago.

So, Nathan hadn't been out yet today. At least that meant she could break the news of the village's defiance on her own terms.

She walked up to the front door. The other boot prints paused by the doorbell, confirming her theory. As she rang the bell herself, she wondered if it might not have been a good idea to bring someone else for moral support. With trees looming over its roof, the house looked gloomier than ever.

The door opened just a moment before she lost her nerve. She looked up to see Nathan standing there, wearing a black sweater and jeans, his handsome face as cold as a block of ice.

'Yes? Do you have a specific reason for not calling ahead? I was in the middle of something.'

His response caught Emily unawares. She hesitated a moment before giving a shrug. 'Phone ran out of charge,' she said.

'Mobile phones,' Nathan said, shaking his head. 'What a terrible additional strain on the National Grid.'

'I scold myself daily,' Emily said, offering a little smile, but receiving only a scowl in response. 'Are you going to let me in, then? I can't imagine the strain on your house's heating system all this cold air is causing.'

With a sigh, he stepped back, allowing her entry. She pulled her boots off in the porch and followed him inside, half wishing he had left the front door open in case she needed to escape.

'Coffee?' he asked as they reached the dining room, where she saw he had been reading the newspaper again. It was open on a double spread paper about an overseas war.

'I'd prefer hot chocolate if you've got it,' Emily said. 'I'm a bit low on sugar this morning. A long night, I'm afraid.'

Nathan scowled. 'I might have some in the back of a cupboard somewhere.'

'A marshmallow or two would be great.'
'What do I look like, Costa Coffee?'
'Costa does them now?'

Nathan scowled again before turning away and heading for the kitchen. Emily glanced at the newspaper one more time, rolling her eyes. Then, while Nathan was still out of sight, she pulled something out of her pocket.

Nathan came back with a steaming mug. He set it down on a coaster in front of her with a brief grunt of approval.

'Godiva,' he said. 'Extra bitter.'

Emily smiled. 'I would expect nothing less.'

Nathan turned to reach for his coffee. Then, noticing the object on the table, he stopped, hand poised tantalisingly in mid-air.

'What's this?'

'It's a gift.'

'I don't—'

Emily shook her head. 'It's wrapped in brown paper and contains no … unwelcome imagery at all. And it's a gift simply to thank you for allowing me to stay at late notice. I was in an uncertain place in my life, and thanks to this trip, I'm feeling much better.'

Nathan continued to stare at it. 'I don't need a gift,' he said.

'It doesn't matter whether you need it or not, I've chosen to give it. And I want you to accept it with good grace, from one person to another.'

His hand moved slowly to pick it up. He turned the small box over in his hands. 'What is it?' he asked.

'Just open it.'

Frowning, he untied the string that wrapped the small brown rectangle, then gently unfolded the paper.

'It's a pen,' he said, turning the box toward her, as if she hadn't already known what it was. 'I have dozens of pens.'

'It's a limited edition Parker,' Emily said. 'But you're right, it is just a pen.'

'Why did you give me a pen?'

'Like I said, to say thank you. You helped me in a way you can't understand.'

'But why a pen? It's almost worthless.'

Emily laughed. After coming off the Skype call with Liselle, she hadn't really believed what Nathan's sister had told her until now. It was clear that Nathan had issues that would take time and effort to resolve.

'What it cost is not what's important. It's what's attached to it. It's what it came wrapped inside.'

'A plastic box with a bit of felt on it.'

'Gratitude.'

Nathan frowned, then gave a slow nod. 'It's not the money, is it?'

'It has nothing to do with money. It could have cost any amount. As it happens, it cost sixteen pounds ninety-nine, but I got four pounds off because I bought two at once, in order to give one to another friend who also helped me out. That's proper money management for you, isn't it?'

Nathan nodded again. He turned the pen over in his hands, like a child receiving a gift for the first time.

'I talked to your sister,' Emily said, playing her trump card.

Nathan's face shot up. 'What?'

'And a few other people, too.'

'Who?'

'Actually, most of the significance is in the people whom I didn't talk to. People who don't exist.'

'What?'

'You have a lot of questions, when you actually have most of the answers. Can I sit down?'

'Sit?'

Emily pointed at the nearest chair. 'It would be you offering kindness to my weary legs,' she said.

'Sit,' Nathan said again. 'Please.'

'I came here both to thank you, and to inform you,' Emily said. 'I know you're wealthy, and I know how that feels. But money isn't power, and it doesn't give you the right to control other people.'

For the first time Nathan's eyes flared with anger. 'You talk about money as though it's nothing,' he said. 'I'm worth several million pounds—'

Emily laughed. 'And it makes you feel empty, doesn't it? You never have to work again, yet you're still young. You're what, thirty?'

'Thirty-three,' Nathan said. 'You can't possibly understand—'

'I'm twenty-nine,' Emily interrupted, putting up a hand. 'You think you're the only one with money?' She rolled her eyes. 'When my grandmother died in October, she not only left me her business, but a rather unexpected surprise.'

Nathan blinked. For the first time, Emily knew she had truly surprised him. Seeing the number on the legal document still shocked her. It had taken several phone calls to convince her they hadn't made a mistake.

'My grandmother was a remarkable woman,' Emily said. 'She had a successful business and she was a pillar of the community, but not only that, when she was barely older than I am now, she built from scratch a windmill energy system capable of powering an entire home. She got a patent on it, and selling the rights to its development to various companies across the world made her very wealthy indeed. So I know exactly what it feels like to never have to work again. I could sit on my bum watching TV and eating pizzas for the rest of my life and I'd still die with a fortune in the bank. It's a weird feeling, but after coming to Cottonwood, I realised that wealth doesn't give you the right to hold power over people. It's a privilege, one that allows you to give back so much more.' She took a sip of hot chocolate, wincing at the bitterness. It was like he had added a couple of spoonfuls of coffee just to flush out any hint of sugar.

'I came to Cottonwood because I found a letter,' Emily continued. 'The letter asked for someone to bring back Christmas. You see, while Christmas might seem tacky to some people—after all, what gift could anyone possibly buy someone with your or my money that we couldn't just buy ourselves?—it means different things to different people. For some, it's about hope. Others it's togetherness, and for others it's about holding out the deep, dark world for a few short weeks. It means something to people, and no one has the right to take that away.'

Nathan, who had sat quietly throughout Emily's

speech, said nothing. He turned to his newspaper, turning the page to reveal another war report.

'So much misery in the world,' he said. 'Why try to hide behind an illusion?'

Emily shook her head. 'Don't pull that one on me,' she said. 'If you thought that, you'd grudgingly accept it, whether you liked it or not. I haven't forgotten how you reacted to the cake I brought you.'

Nathan shifted on his chair, clearly unsettled.

'I talked to your sister,' Emily reminded him. 'She told me what happened when you were little.'

Nathan shook his head. 'No. I can't talk about that.'

Emily reached into her pocket and pulled out Mrs. Taylor's card. 'I'm not asking you to. Not to me at any rate. This is a card for Claudette Taylor, who lives up the road. She's a retired clinical psychiatrist. I asked her if you could talk to her about your fear of Christmas. She said to call her anytime at all.'

Nathan didn't move. Emily put the card down on the table next to his newspaper. 'The option's there,' she said. 'I'd also be happy to talk to you, but I'm not a professional. All I can do is listen. You know where I am, though. Come by whenever you like.'

She stood up, and made her way out. At the front door she looked back. Nathan was still sitting where she had left him, staring at the card on the table.

'Good luck,' Emily whispered, before letting herself out.

28
ANTICIPATION

It was snowing heavily as Emily made her way back to the holiday let, more than twenty centimetres now where the snow had been untouched. Inside, she found Veronica together with Graham from the council jovially slapping chocolate icing on a line of chocolate logs while singing along to Christmas songs.

'Going well?' she asked.

'Not bad,' Veronica said. 'What's up?'

'Just visited Trower,' Emily answered.

'Ooh, Skeletor? How'd that go? He melt you with his laser eyes?'

'I made it out alive,' Emily said. 'I'm pretty sure he's not going to sabotage anything. At least, no more than he has done already.'

'That's good to know.'

If she were honest with herself, Emily still felt a little uncomfortable with the way her meeting with Nathan Trower had gone. It felt too passive, as though she had got off lightly. This was a man who had manipulated and lied in order to squeeze the life out of an entire village for more than two years. Was the simple gift of a cheap pen and a talking to going to make him change his ways?

She shook her head. Not likely.

'Are you good with finishing these?' she asked Veronica.

The girl cracked Graham on the shoulder. 'Perfectly. Did you know he used to be professional pub singer? He's note perfect on most of these songs.'

'Is there such a thing?' Emily asked, as Graham looked up from the cake he was icing and smiled.

'But you know, don't tell Peter, eh. Just in case.'

'I'm married with two kids,' Graham said. 'Don't worry, you're safe.'

Veronica started blushing. 'I didn't mean it like that—'

Emily put up a hand. 'I'll leave you two to figure things out,' she said.

∼

Keeping busy was the only way to settle her nerves. Outside her gate, the entire village had turned into a production line of preparations, from the fairy lights stringing up along the church yard fence to the snacks and drinks stalls setting up outside local businesses. Outside the shop, Emily found Skip helping Peter to drag a popcorn machine out onto the pavement.

'Not sure if it still works,' Peter said. 'Mum said we had one out the back, but I didn't believe her. It was under an old blanket.'

'What we're thinking is that Monday's carnival procession will do a loop of the village green, before making its way up to the village hall car park,' Skip said. 'A reversal of the route it used to take before Trower stopped us using the green.'

Emily, who had fought enough battles with Nathan already and had decided to leave his claim of ownership to the village green for another day, nodded. 'Sounds like a good idea,' she said.

'And while people are waiting to get going, they'll need popcorn, right?' Peter said.

'And beer,' Skip added.

'I think you guys are on top of it,' Emily said.

Peter had looked up, but now he frowned as he looked past her. Emily turned to see Veronica coming out of the holiday let with Graham trailing behind her, carrying a tray, its contents hidden by a towel.

'Who's that guy Veronica's with?' Peter asked.

Emily laughed. 'That's Graham. He works for the council. Don't worry, he's married with two kids.'

'I was just asking.' Peter, his cheeks flushed with more than the exertion of moving the popcorn machine, tried to hide his face as Veronica and Graham reached them.

'Saw you out the window,' Veronica said. 'Snack time.'

'Thanks,' Skip said. 'If you like, I'll open up the bar and we can get out of the snow.'

'What's this?' Emily asked.

'Choco log and coffee,' Veronica said.

'But we need these for—'

Veronica put up a hand. 'Tester,' she said. 'And the coffee's my own blend. Another tester.'

'Let's go then.'

Graham, still carrying the tray, followed Skip over to the pub. Veronica and Peter exchanged glances while Emily stood awkwardly in the middle.

'All right?' Peter asked.

'All right?' Veronica answered.

'Yeah.'

'Yeah. Ah, thanks for the help last night.'

'No problem.'

'You, ah, wanna come get coffee later?'

'Sure. And we've got one to drink now, haven't we.'

'Oh, yeah.'

'Cool.'

Emily smiled. 'I'll see you guys inside,' she said. Veronica shot her a don't-you-dare-leave-me look, but Emily just winked and headed after Skip and Graham. Inside, she found them setting up the drinks and cake on a table. Skip had switched on the TV, which was playing a Christmas movie, and turned on the lights to reveal he had done his own decorating: a beautiful tree laden with decorations now lit up one corner.

'Nice,' Emily said.

'Well, it is Christmas,' Skip answered. 'Got to get into the spirit of it all, haven't we?'

∼

An hour later, after a pleasant time eating, drinking,

and watching Veronica and Peter adorably fumble through one conversation after another, Emily excused herself, returning to the welcome quiet of her holiday let. Despite the upheaval in the garden, temporarily hidden by a blanket of snow, the rest of the house was a sanctuary, protecting her against the racing excitement of the outside world. Veronica and Graham had done an expert job of cleaning the kitchen, the remaining chocolate logs boxed up and left on the work surface. Emily got herself a glass of water and retired to the living room sofa.

The fire was cold in the grate, so she draped a blanket over her knees, not wanting the fuss of starting it. Her laptop was on the coffee table nearby, so she pulled it onto her lap and browsed through local news sites, wondering if Trower had set into action any new sabotage plans.

So far, so good. A couple of notifications had gone out to local press websites, advertising the charity event, although with the roads likely to be icy Emily wasn't sure how many people would be able to make it. News websites were already urging people to stay at home if they could. She had sent an email to a local bus company to ask about hiring a bus to do a park-and-ride service from the nearest council car park, but hadn't yet heard back. Although their website claimed that all-weather services were available, she expected that in practice they wanted to keep their buses locked up during heavy snow. And without such a service, Cottonwood's carnival was limited to those who lived in walking distance: by Emily's estimation about three hundred people.

Whether they got the numbers to justify its charity event status or not, the carnival had done a fine job of pulling people together. Emily logged on to her social media accounts and discovered she had been added to a new Facebook group for Cottonwood, and even been made an admin. Scanning the list of members, Nathan Trower was noticeable by his absence.

She reminded herself it was probably just as well, even though she couldn't help but feel that even in her attempt to rehabilitate him, she had only isolated him further. She wondered if he had given Mrs. Taylor a call yet, but it had only been a couple of hours. It was probably best to leave it all alone for a while.

Still, there were no signs of sabotage that she could see. Unable to resist, she loaded a couple of national listings websites and checked the reviews for all the local businesses she could think of, including her own grandmother's teahouse. No obvious troll reviews. Neither were there any new articles slating any of them. It was as though Nathan Trower had quietly accepted that his lid of Christmas oppression had finally been lifted.

But had he really given up? Emily shook her head, unable to shake a nervous anticipation that Trower was far from beaten, and that despite all the good that was going on, things were about to take a turn for the worse.

29

NIGHT WALKER

Her little car was an overseas import with four-wheel-drive, and Elaine had insisted every year that Emily change the tyres to expensive winter ones, a practice common in Europe and other parts of the world which had a proper winter, but not so much here in England. However, as she carefully negotiated the snowy road out of the village she felt none of the nervousness most drivers felt as they crunched over fresh snow. Elaine had needed deliveries done at all times of the year, and in the past few years that had been Emily's responsibility. Within a few minutes she had made her way out of the icy tangle of roads surrounding Cottonwood and was driving steadily along a far less snowy duel carriageway.

Despite speed restrictions and a couple of spun cars slowing things down, Emily made it back to the teahouse just after lunch. Here in Birchtide the passing storm had left only a sprinkling of snow compared to the heavy fall it had unleashed on

Cottonwood to the south. Emily parked in the driveway and walked up to the teahouse, feeling a little lonesome at how forlorn and abandoned it looked. Despite the cold, weeds had sprung up around the entrance steps—something Elaine would never have allowed—and the windows were beginning to collect a layer of grime.

When she reached the door, she found several former regulars had voiced their frustrations in the form of messages taped to the glass. *We need our cakes! How long are you going to keep us waiting?!* read one particularly irate message. While the events in Cottonwood had restored part of the confidence lost with Elaine's death, now Emily felt the old doubts creeping in. Could she be true to her grandmother's memory? Perhaps she really should do the unthinkable, and sell up, allow another owner to make their mark. It wasn't like she needed the money.

She stared at the messages until the cold began to creep under her jacket. Finally she headed inside, picking up the huge pile of unopened Christmas cards on the mat. She filed through them, checking mostly for bills and messages from suppliers. She would pay or answer them all, keep Elaine's slate clean until she was ready. Maybe that time was soon, maybe not. Emily's stomach felt knotted at the thought of the decision she needed to make.

It was in the loft where she found what she had come for. A collection of earthenware bowls covered with greaseproof paper held down with elastic bands looked like a giant honeycomb when viewed in the light of Emily's phone. Elaine's yearly collection of

Christmas puddings, made every January and left to mature in the loft until December. Emily counted thirty in all, then began carrying them down the stairs and out to the car. She had made a decision about a stall she herself would run, and the puddings were a necessary addition. However, unable to shake a feeling that she was getting rid of a final part of her grandmother, she left the last few in place. If she did decide to reopen, they would still be perfectly edible in a year's time.

Her car felt loaded down with twenty-five Christmas puddings on the floor and in the boot. After a brief stop at a supermarket for a few more bits and bobs she couldn't buy locally, she headed back. The day had got away from her again, and twilight had come as she took the Cottonwood turning off the duel carriageway. The country lanes, formerly a snowy wonderland, took on a grim iciness in the gloom beneath the setting sun. Pulling up out of a valley over a frozen ford, Emily felt her wheels spin before gripping and launching her forward, only for another patch of ice to catch her front tyres and angle her toward the hedge.

She caught herself just in time, but the journey had certainly become a challenge. She threw all her thoughts aside and concentrated on the road ahead, leaning low over the wheel as the car crunched over snow turned hard.

The forest fell away behind her, the sky lightening with one last cast of daylight before the sun set. Emily pulled round a corner, past a small side turning, only to find the road blocked by a fallen tree. Frustrated, she left the car idling and climbed out, wondering if she could perhaps move it. However, while it only looked like a sapling, it was far too heavy and its branches had become entangled with the hedgerow it had fallen upon. Alan likely had some cutting equipment, but Emily would have to go around.

She got back into her car and reversed up the road, taking the side turning. Unplowed, the car could only move at a few miles per hour as Emily bumped over the hardened snow, the wheels spinning and jerking with each undulation. She passed a gateway and saw a line of houses at the top of a snowy field, the village so close she could almost touch it. The road, however, wound back downhill, passing below her own holiday let, then a while later Nathan Trower's place almost hidden by a rear screen of trees. Then, after the last gateway had passed behind her, she descended down into forest.

In the icy gloom parted only by her headlights, she might as well have been in the wilds of Siberia, a million miles away from the joyous preparations for a Christmas event. The road ran on and on, and while the snow was less under the trees, in places, where snowmelt had run across the road and frozen, her car slipped and slid, only ever a couple of feet away from getting stuck in a ditch.

'Come on,' she muttered to herself, trying to summon the spirit of the snow-loving Reverend Billingham. 'Shouldn't I be enjoying this?'

She turned a corner, wheels spinning, and found herself heading back uphill. In the far distance, her headlights illuminated the silhouette of a man walking along the road. As a matter of habit she reached across and pressed down the door locks, but as she got closer, she became more certain that it was Nathan Trower, out walking in the dark.

Emily shook her head. The man was an enigma. Down here in the forest, on the icy roads beneath the gloom, he was walking with his hands in his pockets and with no sign of a torch. Without her car lights he would be walking in near darkness, yet he was moving with an ease that suggested he felt no concern at all.

He appeared to walk faster as she gradually gained on him, briefly disappearing around a corner before reappearing up ahead a minute later as Emily made the turn. They were out of the woods now, but the light had almost gone, and through her side windows the towering hedgerows were dark sentinels.

How Trower knew where he was going, Emily guessed came down to a lifelong familiarity with the area. She felt similar about Birchtide, recognising the outline of trees, gateways, the angle of the road, even in the dark. Even so, on a night like this she would have been curled up on the sofa watching the TV.

Finally Emily came to a crossroads where a slightly larger road led back to the village. Trower should have turned left, his own house just half a mile back along the road, but to Emily's surprise he headed straight across, taking the road which led around to Rowe Farm. As Emily made the turn, she frowned at the last sight of him, walking fast, head bowed, hands in his pockets. Despite her car trailing him for the last half a mile, he hadn't turned back to look, not once.

It was as though he had other things on his mind.

30

OPTIMISM

Too tired to cook, Emily headed over to the Inn on the Green to look for something for dinner, where she found Skip hastily blowing the cobwebs out of the long-unused kitchens in preparation for the upcoming carnival. Veronica was also there, along with another local lady called Stephanie Goddard, who Veronica had said owned the small art supplies shop. Together they had been trying—unsuccessfully—to coax an old electric cooker back to life.

'It used to work,' Skip said. 'Always took a while to warm up, though.'

'You got it plugged in?' Veronica asked.

'I think so,' Skip said, kneeling on the floor to peer into the gloom between the cooker's feet and the floor.

'I imagine the mouse chewed through the wire,' Stephanie said with a smirk, provoking a sharp glare from Veronica.

'Mice?'

'It's a joke.'

'Hope so. Saw one once. Still get nightmares.'

'Been so long since I cooked anything in here there's nothing for them to eat,' Skip said. 'I'll see if I can get an engineer out in the morning to have a look. Dinner's a no-go then.'

'Let's go round Peter's for beans on toast,' Veronica said, the insistence in her voice making it impossible to refuse.

The others looked at each other then gave a collective shrug. 'Why not?' Skip said. 'I'll put a bit of card in the window to say we're closed up for a couple of hours.'

With Veronica taking the lead, they headed next door. Peter answered her sharp knock, his face immediately brightening at the sight of Veronica, multi-coloured hair flecked with snow, standing on his doorstep.

'Beans offer still open?' she asked. 'Skip's cooker flaked on the fish n' chips.'

'Good timing,' Peter said. 'We just found a rack of plastic chairs out in the garage.'

Peter led them inside. In a large dining room at the back of the house, they found a crowd already assembled. In addition to a handful of people whose names Emily couldn't recall, the three council workers were there, as was Mrs. Taylor, and even Reverend Billingham.

'Skip, is that you?' Kelly called from an adjoining kitchen. 'Do you have a spare toaster over there? I'm good for bread, but cooking it is proving a little difficult.'

Skip glanced at Veronica, who shrugged.

'There was one in the cupboard by the door,' Stephanie said. 'It'll probably work if you blow the rust off.'

'I'll be right back,' Skip said.

'And bring a few Cokes,' Kelly called.

'Sure.'

∽

With Emily helping Kelly to prepare a huge vat of baked beans, the group enjoyed a jovial evening eating and drinking in Kelly's back room. They opened a couple of windows to let a breeze keep the air clean as the beans started to do their work, but everyone was in good spirits ahead of the opening of the carnival in two days' time. Emily got an update from those people working at the site that the village hall was nearly ready. All decorations were in place, and the local stalls were all set up. Tomorrow would see the arrival of a couple of special vendors, plus the sound and disco equipment. With snow still steadily falling, Alan had promised to be up clearing the roads early to make sure everyone could arrive on time, while Garry Timpson was on standby with his Land Rover to pick up anyone who got stuck.

Later on, after everyone had headed back over to the pub for a nightcap, Emily managed to get a word with Mrs. Taylor.

'Has Nathan Trower called you?' she asked.

Mrs. Taylor nodded. 'Yes, he called me this afternoon,' she said. 'We had a little chat over the phone, but he's going to come over tomorrow morning for a chat face to face. I'm afraid I can't really talk about what he said—patient confidentiality and all that—but let's just say that he's hoping to change his ways.'

'So you think he'll let the carnival go off without any problems?'

Mrs. Taylor patted Emily on the shoulder. 'After all your hard work, I'd hate to see something bad happen, but I'm confident it won't. I'm not sure whether he'd be there doing Christmas karaoke, but I think he understands that what he's been doing was wrong. He has some issues, that boy, but I think there's light at the end of the tunnel. I don't think you quite realise what an impact you've had on everyone round here.'

Emily shrugged. 'Just trying to answer a letter,' she said.

∼

It was nearly midnight when she returned to the holiday let. Exhausted, all she wanted was to hit her bed, but she made herself go through every room, checking for any unwanted Easter eggs, half expecting to find a box of cockroaches or snakes under her bed. She found nothing untoward, however. Perhaps Mrs. Taylor was right and Nathan really had seen the error of his ways.

Just as she was climbing into bed, her phone buzzed with a message from Karen.

Gonna snow heavily tomorrow. Take it easy in the snow.

You need a lift, give me a shout and I'll send out the butler with the minibus. It's built like a tank.

Emily had a sudden flash of inspiration. *Do you think I could borrow it for a couple of days?*

The butler or the tank? His name's Archibald and he's seventy, but if you can look past the barcode he makes with his last remaining hair then I guess he's nice-looking enough.

The tank.

I thought so.

You're a life saver. Love you x.

You too x.

Emily grinned as she lay back on her pillows. She now had a way to get people in to the carnival and out again. Perfect. Things were looking up.

As her eyes started to close, despite a million other things she probably should be doing, perhaps the most important question of all rushed to the front of her mind.

She hadn't even thought about it until now, but it really was of utmost importance.

Her costume for the upcoming carnival.

What on earth was she going to wear?

31

LOST IN THE SNOW

As soon as she got out of bed, Emily took a walk up to the village hall to check on preparations. A few people were already there, looking bleary-eyed after a long night in the pub, clearing out their hangovers by digging the fresh snow out of the car park. Karen had been right; it had dumped overnight, with nearly twenty centimetres of fresh snow. Cottonwood was looking a lot more cotton wool, with huge drifts alongside the roads where people had piled it up.

Walking back down to her place, she passed Alan on his tractor, already out plowing the roads. He gave her a wave and shouted Merry Christmas, and for a moment she thought about asking for a ride on the tractor before remembering she had a list of tasks to do. Alan had opened up the gates of a couple of empty fields in order to have somewhere to put the collected snow, and she stood and watched for a couple of minutes as he drove a huge drift through an entrance, pushing it up against a load nearly ten feet high, before backing his tractor out again.

Back in the main square she found Skip and Peter out clearing the snow in front of the shop and the pub, the popcorn machine whirring as it ran a test load.

'Got the cooker working!' Skip called by way of greeting, and Emily gave him a thumbs-up as she did a circle of the village green. Something looked different about it today, and it wasn't just because of the thick covering of snow.

Something was missing.

It took her a moment to realise. The sign restricting access was gone. Where it had stood, there were a few scuffle marks in the snow, followed by a line of half-covered footprints leading off the green and back up the road in the direction of Trower's house.

Emily couldn't hold back a smile. Nathan really had changed his ways.

With one last look at the green, she headed back into her holiday let, made herself a coffee and set to work with the long list of phone calls she had to make.

First she had to call Karen and confirm the loan of the minibus, after which she needed to rush out a couple of adverts to local news sites. A phone call and a bit of a beg to a local supermarket manager established a base for a park-and-ride, provided the supermarket could provide an advertising board and a few boxes of own-brand mince pies. Despite having charged Veronica with making a couple of hundred this morning, they would provide a useful backup.

Everything was going swimmingly. With less than forty-eight hours until the opening ceremony, nearly everything was in place. All they needed to do was stockpile food and drinks and check everything was working.

Emily was just wondering whether a corner of Christmas pudding and a glass of wine would pass off as a sufficient lunch when she heard a frantic knock at the door.

She answered it to find Veronica standing there, looking awkward. 'Bit of a prob,' the girl said. 'Kid's gone missing.'

Emily felt a hot flush rush over her. 'What?'

'Alan Rowe's kid.'

She pulled on her boots and followed Veronica out into the square. A group of people were gathering outside the pub. Emily recognised Skip, Kelly and Peter, Stephanie, Leon from the council crew, and the Benson couple—Mark and Jane—who lived two doors up from the village hall.

'Here's Alan now,' Skip said, pointing as the tractor came rumbling into view.

Moving far faster than he should have been, Alan ground the machine to a halt beside the green and jumped down.

'I've been right down to the river,' he said. 'Nothing. He knows not to go farther than that.' He shook his head, and Emily could see he was holding back tears. 'I've called the police and they said they'd send someone out as soon as they could, but in this weather….' He took a deep breath. 'I don't know.'

Emily stepped forward. 'Fill me in,' she said, a couple of other new arrivals nodding too. 'What's going on?'

'John took the dog out,' Alan said. 'He always does of a morning, but in this snow he knows to stick to the lane and come back. He's been gone nearly three hours. Barbara was trying to call me, but I was down the valley with the tractor where there's no reception.' He shook his head again. 'I've done a complete circuit, clearing out the roads, but there's no sign of him. No tracks, nothing.'

'We'll get the village together,' Skip said. 'He can't have gone far.'

Alan looked so distraught he could barely answer. He turned his head, peering up at the sky. 'It'll start getting dark in a couple of hours. I couldn't bear to lose him … not after … not after….'

He trailed off. Emily felt a sudden urge to go to him, but Kelly, standing closer, put an arm around his shoulders. 'I'm sure John's fine,' she said. 'You know what kids are like. He probably just went exploring in the snow.'

'Not my John. Not without telling me.'

'I've put a new update on the social page,' Stephanie said, holding up her phone. 'I said for everyone who's free to meet us here.' She looked down at her phone, then frowned. 'Oh dear. Bad news, I'm afraid.'

'What?'

'There's another tree come down just before the

Uglow Ford. Ben Marsh from Wake Dean House said there's a police car down there, but it's gone into a ditch. They've called for a breakdown truck, but it could be hours.'

'I don't have time to waste,' Alan snapped. 'My boy is out there. I have to get back out there looking for him.'

He pushed away from Kelly and walked a few paces up the road before turning and coming back, uncertain what to do.

'I've got a map of the parish inside,' Skip said. 'We'll split into groups, take a road each. One group head down to Uglow Ford, let the police know what we're up to, and then follow the footpath along the river to the junction below Tingles Hill. He can't have gone far.'

Almost as an act of defiance, the snowfall suddenly increased its intensity. Emily looked across at the church but could barely see beyond the gate. She looked around at the others, dismayed to see the same doubt in their faces. The temperature was only a degree or two below zero, but would certainly drop after sunset, and in this snow visibility would be next to nothing. If they weren't careful, other people could get lost.

'We'll find him,' Kelly said. 'We'll comb the whole parish if we have to.'

Alan said nothing. He gripped the sides of his head as though unable to handle the thoughts contained inside.

'You're wasting your time,' said a new voice from behind them. Emily turned. Nathan Trower was walking up the road, a rucksack slung over his back, a cold, hard look on his face.

A tension fell over the group. Emily looked from one face to another. This was it, she realised, the moment they had all feared but hoped would never come. The moment when the dragon which had spent the last two years draining the life out of the village finally raised its head and opened its eyes to the rebellion going on around it—a rebellion it could crush with one dramatic sweep of its tail.

For a moment the only sound was the gentle patter of snow punctuated by Trower's crunching footfalls as he approached. Emily could only stare. Beside her, Veronica slipped her hand into Peter's while Stephanie linked her arm through Skip's and the Bensons hugged against each other.

Nathan was within ten steps when the tension exploded.

'What have you done with my boy?' Alan roared, launching himself forward. He might have made it to Nathan had his boots not slipped in the snow, giving Skip just enough time to get between them. 'What have you done with him?' Alan shouted again as Skip struggled to keep the strong farmer's fists at his sides. 'I'll—'

Nathan lifted his hands. 'Nothing,' he said. 'I haven't done a thing.'

'You're a liar!'

Nathan shook his head. 'I read your message on that group,' he said. 'The first one about twenty minutes ago, about John not coming home? You know, on that group I'm supposed to be blocked from? You need to fix your privacy controls.'

'So you came to gloat, did you, Nathan?' Skip said.

Nathan shook his head. 'I came to help.'

'We don't need your help,' Stephanie snapped.

'Get out of here,' Kelly added.

'Wait.' Emily put up a hand. 'We're not animals. Let him speak. Let's hear what he has to say.'

Nathan gave her a brief look—one of thanks, perhaps?—then dropped his rucksack from his shoulders and pulled out a box.

'My drone,' he said.

'What?' Alan rolled his eyes. He pushed Skip off him and stalked a few steps away. 'You're a fool. We're standing around talking to this idiot when my son's out there, missing.'

'It has a heat sensor,' Nathan said. 'You won't find anything with cameras in this blizzard, but my drone will pick up heat.'

Alan looked skeptical, but the others were looking from one to another.

'If he's had a fall, if he's hurt, you could walk within a couple of steps of him and not see him in this snow, but my drone can detect the body heat of small animals. If he's out there, it'll find him.'

'It's worth a try,' Emily said.

'Can we get out of the snow?' Nathan said, even after everything his voice holding a level of dismissiveness which Emily could tell raised a few hackles. 'This is expensive equipment.'

'Into the pub,' Skip said.

Nathan followed Skip inside with the others trailing along behind. Nathan pulled a laptop out of his bag and set it up on a table. The drone was in a box. No more than thirty centimetres across, it was an elegant chrome quad-copter that looked expensive.

'That's the thing you've been using to spy on me, is it?' Emily said with a wry smile.

Nathan didn't return it. 'You and the rest of the village,' he said, his expression still cold. 'It has a heat sensor, as well as night vision, and an automatic obstacle avoidance feature which will make it maneuverable beneath the trees. We just need to set up its locator to GPS.'

'Looks pricy,' Skip quipped.

'It's worth about as much as this pub,' Nathan answered, not looking up. Skip just rolled his eyes. He looked about to say something in response, but decided to keep it to himself. Even though Nathan had emerged from his isolation and offered to help, he still looked as though he'd rather be anywhere else.

A map appeared on the screen with a flashing dot in its centre. Nathan nodded, then took the machine out of its box and put it down on the tabletop.

'Open the door,' he said. 'I'll operate it from here.'

He took a controller out of the box while Stephanie held the door for Kelly to prop it open with a wedge. Nathan pressed a switch on the quad-copter's underside and the room filled with an unpleasant buzzing as the four upper propellers began to spin.

'Stand back, please.'

Everyone got out of the way as Nathan pressed a button and the quad-copter rose gently into the air.

'Checking cameras,' Nathan said as the computer screen split to reveal a view of the bar. As the machine slowly spun around, the view took in the stunned group of adults.

'That's how they work, is it?' Skip said.

'Checking heat sensor,' Nathan said. The picture switched from a regular video to a series of red splotches. 'Okay, we're good.' He pressed another control and the quad-copter sped out of the main door, the image on the screen turning into a blur.

'I have two hours of battery,' Nathan said. 'Let's hope your boy didn't go too far. We'll check along the main roads of the village, then we'll start sweeping the fields and forests. The drone has a maximum speed of eighty miles per hour, so we can cover a lot of ground quickly.'

Alan nodded. 'I really appreciate this,' he said.

Nathan looked up at him. For a few seconds Emily wondered if he would say something profound, but he just returned the nod. 'I'm just glad I could help,' he said.

They gathered around Nathan as the drone moved slowly over the map, at first following the roads that made a sewing box tangle of the local area, but when they found nothing, Nathan pointed at a patch of contour lines with a thicker line in the middle.

'This is the stream down from Uglow Ford,' he said. 'Probably the most dangerous place in the village during this kind of weather. We'll check along there first.'

Moving slower to account for the trees, the drone made its way along the route of the river. A couple of red dots appeared, provoking a gasp from Alan, but Nathan said they were too small to be people. Most likely rabbits out braving the conditions.

As they moved deeper into the forest, the tension began to rise. On the split screen video view there was little to see other than falling snow and the occasional dark shadow of a tree trunk.

Then—

'There!' Nathan shouted, punching the tabletop in a rare outlet of emotion. 'We've got two readings, one larger than the other.'

'John and the dog,' Alan said. 'Are you sure?'

'Let's go in closer and have a better look,' Nathan said.

The group crowded around Nathan's shoulders as he switched the view over to a full screen video. At first all that could be seen was a white blur of falling snow, but then something blue appeared. As it increased in size, it took shape as a person, crouched down.

'That's his rain jacket,' Alan said. 'Is he all right?'

The camera zoomed closer. The shape, disturbed by the drone's noise, shifted. A head rose, and John's face peered out from under a hood. This close, it was possible to see the frown on his face. One arm was holding Winston against him, but the other lifted to give a tentative wave.

Nathan grinned. 'He's sheltering from the storm. Go and get him.'

'I know exactly where that is,' Alan said, already heading for the door.

'If he's hurt, we might not be able to get an ambulance in,' Skip said. 'Are there any doctors in the village?'

'There's Phil Woodhall, who lives behind the church,' Jane Benson said.

'Someone go and get him,' Skip said. 'Meet us at Rowe Farm.'

Alan asked for a few people to go with him in case it took some effort to get John and the dog out. Peter and Ted Benson immediately put up their hands. Aware that Barbara and Lily might not know what was going on, Emily volunteered to go straight to Rowe Farm and prepare them.

As she headed for the door she turned to look at Nathan, who was still hunched over the laptop, keeping the drone in place.

'Thank you,' she said.

When he looked up, he gave a little smile.

32

RECOVERY

John was cold and a bit shaken up, but, according to Dr. Woodhall, a retired GP who willingly left his television to trudge through the snow to Rowe Farm, he would be fine. There were no signs of hypothermia, and his advice was a lot of rest, food, and plenty of Christmas TV.

Beneath the trees, the footpaths had been relatively clear of snow, so Alan and his team had managed to get both John and Winston out without too much trouble. John, who had lost the path in the snow and decided to wait the blizzard out until it stopped, had been a bit shaken up. Winston, on the other hand, had loved every minute of it, and within ten minutes of being back at the house he was scratching at the door to be let back out.

'We often go down to the river,' John told Emily as he sat clutching a cup of hot chocolate on the edge of the sofa. Lily sat beside him, watching a Postman Pat Christmas Special on TV. Winston, having finally calmed down, lay beside her, barking at the screen every time Postman Pat's cat appeared.

'I suppose it looked a bit different in the snow,' Emily said.

John nodded. 'I feel so stupid. Winston chased a rabbit and I got confused about where we were. I thought the snow would just stop in the end and we could get back out.'

Alan came out of the kitchen. He passed another cup of coffee to Emily, then ruffled his son's hair. 'You did good, son,' he said. 'Might be best to keep Winston on a lead and stick to the roads until the weather's cleared.'

'I will, Dad. Can I still go to the Christmas carnival?'

Emily looked up at Alan, who lifted an eyebrow. 'You're the guest of honour,' he said. 'You're not missing that carnival for anything.'

'Can I be the guest of honour too?' Lily asked.

Emily laughed. 'Sure you can. It's Christmas, isn't it?'

∽

The other villagers had already left, but Emily stayed on to help Alan prepare dinner. Still visibly shaken up by the thought of losing his son, he was like a headless chicken, picking things up and putting them down again, turning around in circles, blathering inanely about nothing of importance until Emily finally put up a hand.

'Look,' she said, patting him on the shoulder,

before suddenly realising what she had done and pulling her hand away. Composing herself, she continued, 'Look, I have an idea. I'll get something done for dinner. You and the kids get some proper Christmas decorations up.'

'We already did.'

Emily shook her head. 'You call a tiny Christmas tree in the hall and a wreath on the inside of the door decorating? I bet you have boxes of stuff in a cupboard somewhere.'

Alan shrugged. 'We have the old tree we used to put in the living room before Katherine passed.'

'Go and get it.'

'But don't you need some help?'

'I have a professional chef's qualification. I'll be fine.'

'All right.'

As he headed off, Emily thought about what she had just said. It had just popped out, intended as a joke. However, it was also true, something Elaine had insisted on as part of her training. Now that she thought about it, she had a lot of things. A diploma in business, certificates in hygiene, food preparation, even in accounting and tax management.

Elaine had prepared her well.

'You knew, didn't you?' Emily whispered as she started chopping carrots. 'You knew one day you'd leave me with everything. You were making sure I was ready.'

It had never been something they discussed. Until Elaine's will was opened, Emily had been unsure what would happen to the teahouse, nor the extent of her grandmother's fortune. While twenty percent of Elaine's substantial monetary assets—roughly two million pounds—had been left to a variety of local charities, including a children's home, a homeless shelter, and a refuge for abandoned pets, the rest had gone solely to Emily.

The money alone was enough to set Emily up for life, but she understood a few things now.

You were the sum of your parts, not the sum of your numbers. It was easy to say that money wasn't important when you had an awful lot of it, but the ability to use it to hollow you out and leave you as a shell lacquered with silver and gold didn't mean you had to do it. A lot of zeros at the end of a bank statement or a big and powerful car couldn't replace an act of kindness, a needed smile, a reassuring word.

She dropped the carrots into a pot and set them to boil. Behind her, she heard laughter, followed by rapid barking, and turned to see Winston had somehow managed to get himself tangled in a piece of tinsel and was now dragging a plastic Christmas tree across the living room. Alan and the kids were trying to corner the playful dog, in order to untangle both him and the tree, but Winston, leaping from chair to chair, was having none of it. As the dog made a dart for the door out into the hall, Alan gave Emily a frantic wave.

'I don't suppose you could spare a minute to block off an escape route or two?' he asked.

Emily laughed. 'I'll be right there,' she said.

33

COSTUMES AND EXPLANATIONS

Saturday morning greeted Emily with bright, clear skies as she took a coffee and sat outside on the back patio, using a towel to first wipe a layer of snow off the table and chair. Even though the blizzard had cleared overnight, the air temperature was still a couple of degrees below zero and the snow showed no sign of going anywhere. With more forecast for this evening—though not quite the same amount as yesterday—it looked like the Christmas carnival would play out in beautiful wintry conditions.

Today was the final day of preparations before tomorrow's carnival. Emily felt both relieved and excited, partly for the event itself, but also for the challenges that were coming on the horizon. In three days, the carnival would be over, her work here would be done, and she would need to face what she had been running from all this time.

She had already decided what she would do.

With a blanket over her knees, the view down

across the snow-covered garden and of the valley beyond was worth braving the cold. She got up to get herself another coffee, but had only just made it to the kettle when someone knocked on the door.

It was just after eight o'clock, so Emily expected work was already underway up at the carnival site. Today the last stalls should be setting up, while mobile toilets and a first aid stand were expected later on. She had handed over much of the supervision to Kelly and Skip, but perhaps she was needed for something she had overlooked.

Just about the last thing she was expecting to find standing on her doorstep was Cinderella, resplendent in a gold lace ballroom dress, a little golden crown perched on her head, which at first appeared to be twinkling, but on closer inspection was fitted with battery-powered fairy lights.

'Do you think Peter will like it?' Veronica asked.

Emily was too stunned to reply. She just shook her head for a few seconds, then burst out laughing.

'He'll hate it, won't he? I'll take it off. Can you help?'

'Wait, no, just hang on a minute.' Emily glanced up and down the street, finding it empty. 'Quick, get inside before anyone sees you.'

Veronica stumbled through the door, the wire frame that kept the dress's hem extended catching on a stone frog doorstop for a moment before popping free.

'So, this is your costume for the carnival, is it?' Emily said, managing to get Veronica inside and the door finally shut. 'Cinderella?'

Veronica rolled her eyes. 'I'm Tinkerbell,' she said.

'Oh. Well, I guess they're not so different.'

'We decided to go to the carnival together,' Veronica said.

'What's Peter going as?'

Veronica rolled her eyes and groaned as though the answer should have been obvious. 'Peter Pan.'

'Right. I'm sure you'll look great. You thought you'd just test it, did you?'

'Bought it last year for a friend's party,' Veronica said. 'Fancy dress, you know.'

'I thought it might be a bit much for a wedding.'

Veronica shrugged. 'Thought I'd better check it still fit. Put on a bit of weight since last year.'

Emily found that hard to believe, but just smiled anyway. 'Well, it looks like it fits fine. You're getting on with Peter okay, are you?'

Veronica's cheeks turned bright red. 'Um, yeah. Seems like it.'

'I'm happy to hear that.'

Veronica looked uncomfortable for a moment, shifting from foot to foot. Emily wondered how easy it was to go to the toilet with such a monumental dress in the way.

'Just wanted to, you know, say thanks.'

'What for?'

'For showing up.'

'Here?'

'Yeah. Otherwise, I might still be in there—' Veronica hooked a thumb over one shoulder '—and he might still be in there.' The thumb hooked over the other shoulder this time. 'Might never have had a chat, you know.'

'You don't need to thank me. You should thank the person who sent the letter I found.'

'I would if you'd tell me who it was.'

Emily smiled. 'Well, maybe one day. I don't want to embarrass him. Did you and Peter sort things out then?'

Veronica shrugged. 'He said sorry for being a dick when we were kids. And I said sorry for telling him his hair looked crap.'

'You do set quite a standard.'

Veronica shrugged. 'I suppose so. Anyway, thanks. Right, I'd better get back. You got your costume sorted?'

Emily shook her head.

'Well, you'd better hurry up.'

'I will.'

As she helped Veronica out, she wondered what on earth she could wear. It had to be something appropriate. As she closed the door, she glanced across the square at the village green, at the spot where the restriction sign had been as recently as yesterday morning.

She wondered if Nathan had thought about going to the carnival, and if so, what his costume might be.

∽

A couple of hours later, after risking the icy roads, Emily found herself in Exeter city centre. Buzzing with people doing last-minute Christmas shopping, she felt as invisible in the crowds as she felt visible among the sparse population of Cottonwood. In some ways it was a relief, in others she felt disappointed. She was one of just millions, after all, every one of them with their own hopes, fears, dreams, and regrets.

Across a selection of fancy dress shops, she was able to get what she needed. Then, after putting her shopping back in the car, she went to meet Karen for coffee and lunch.

'So glad to see you again,' Karen said. 'I've been drowning in testosterone these last few days. David and his brothers had an archery competition yesterday, for heaven's sake.'

'Who won?'

'The mother-in-law. Would you believe that heinous creature almost made the team for the 1980 Olympics? She pulled a muscle in her crotch the night before the eliminations and had to pull out. She still won four national titles, though.'

'I don't know how you can stomach all that achievement.'

Karen shrugged. 'She hasn't won a game of Uno in three years. Not against me, at any rate.' Leaning forward to lower her voice, she added, 'I always sleeve a couple of plus fours on the shuffle, just to make sure.'

'You're such a rebel. Are you all set for tomorrow?'

'We'll be over there bright and early. Costumes are prepared.'

'What are you going as?'

'Snow White and the seven dwarfs. I had to rock-scissors-paper with the M-I-L for Whitey or the Queen. It was touch and go for a moment there.'

'Who won?'

'She did, of course. Although I've upgraded the queen to Maleficent. More of a feminist vibe. Plus, she's hot.'

'Sounds great. I can't wait.'

'And as well as Archibald manning the minibus, the boys are happy to bring a couple of the Land Rovers to help out with the ferrying of people to and from. Are you expecting many?'

Emily smiled. 'Apparently five hundred people have liked the advertising post on Facebook, so that's positive, isn't it?'

Karen reached across and patted her on the hand. 'You've done a brilliant job,' she said. 'You must be so proud.'

'All I did was nudge them in the right direction. I think they would have got there in the end by themselves eventually.'

'Yeah, in ten years. You're a legend. Now, have you thought about what happens after? What happens to the teahouse?'

Emily nodded. 'Yeah, I have. I think I'm over the grieving stage. It's time to move on with my life.'

~

She stopped by the teahouse on her way back. The place felt empty and unloved, so she got out a mop and bucket and a bottle of window cleaner and spent a couple of hours smartening it up a little. She even hung a string of fairy lights across the front window. She had brought her laptop with her, so when she was done cleaning and tidying she set it up on a table and got to work contacting all Elaine's old suppliers. It took her until mid-afternoon, but with the sky filling with ominous clouds, she was keen to return to Cottonwood before dark.

With the first flurries of snow falling around her as sunset glimmered through the bare branches of nearby trees, she just made it, pulling into her parking space just as the bare gravel began to spot with white.

Skip was standing outside the pub, writing on a chalk board. 'Pre-carnival party for the organising crew,' he shouted across to her. 'All drinks on the house, and I'll be dusting off the karaoke machine. Any time from seven.'

'I'll be there,' Emily called back. 'I can't wait.'

Skip gave her a thumbs-up.

The holiday let was cold, so she spent some time getting a fire going, then went into the kitchen and made herself a bowl of spaghetti for dinner. After another frantic day she had hoped to relax, but since it wasn't likely, she figured she might as well try on her costume to make sure it fitted.

She had just pulled her hands through the sleeves and pulled the hood down over her head when someone knocked on the door.

Emily froze. It might be wise to pretend to be out, so she kept quiet. She waited a full minute, but just as she was certain the visitor had gone, the knock came again.

'I know you're in there,' came Nathan's voice. 'I

haven't been spying on you, but your car is parked across the street and there's smoke coming from the chimney. I just wanted to talk for a couple of minutes.'

While he still sounded like the Nathan she knew, there was something different in his voice. He sounded almost submissive, as though he had finally let his guard down. Emily hurried to the door before he could disappear back into his castle.

'Come in,' she said. 'Sorry, I was just trying on my costume for tomorrow's carnival procession.'

Nathan winced as though it was a personal attack. 'I can see that,' he said. 'Don't worry, this will only take a minute.'

'Thank you for yesterday,' Emily said. 'I mean it. What you did was very kind.'

Was that a hint of colour in Nathan's cheeks? 'I couldn't just ignore it,' Nathan said. 'Of course everyone would assume it was my fault, but I could never hurt someone, much less a child. I'm glad there was something I could do to help.'

'So what was it you wanted to talk about?'

Nathan walked past her into the living room and sat down on the sofa facing the fire. He reached forward and began to rub his hands together. Emily followed him in, but unable to sit, she just stood nearby, waiting for him to speak.

'I was seven years old,' he said, staring into the fire. 'I loved Christmas as much as anyone else, and you know how hard it is for kids at that age to sleep on Christmas Eve. As always, I tried to stay awake to wait for Father Christmas, only to fall asleep as always.'

Emily nodded. 'I remember it well. My grandmother used to give me a bunch of housework jobs to do in order to tire me out.'

Nathan gave a brief, pained smile. 'That year, however, I heard a bump from downstairs. The living room was right beneath my bedroom, and the floor was just wood, so I could always hear the hum of the television, or even when people got up or sat down. I got out of bed, and crept downstairs. I peered around the door into the living room, and there he was, right in front of me.'

'Who? Father Christmas?'

'Right there, holding a big bag which he was filling with presents from under the tree.'

'*Filling?*'

Nathan nodded. 'I didn't realise it at first, but that's exactly what he was doing. Remember, I was seven. Without really knowing what I was thinking, I stepped out into the living room and said, "What are you doing?"'

Nathan shivered. His hands shook as he held them out to the fire. A single tear ran down the side of his cheek.

'He looked up at me, and time seemed to stand still,' Nathan said. 'I should have realised that this wasn't the real Father Christmas, but I was seven. I believed in magic back then, and never for a moment questioned that Father Christmas wasn't a real person who actually came down our chimney every Christmas Eve.' He shook his head, then swiped the tear off the edge of his jaw. 'He literally snarled at me like a dog. Then he said, "Breathe a word about this and you'll never get another present again." I was frozen, unable to respond. He took a step toward me, snapping his teeth, and I bolted. I ran up the stairs, back to my room, and hid under the covers. I didn't sleep a wink the rest of the night, and that Christmas morning I had to be practically hauled downstairs.'

'What happened to the man?'

'A few weeks later a local man got arrested for a series of robberies over the Christmas period. Several witnesses saw him dressed up as Father Christmas, a disguise he used to both hide his identity and blend in. Mine wasn't the only house he robbed that Christmas Eve, but I was the only person to catch him in the act.'

'He got away with your presents?'

Nathan shook his head. 'No. That's the worst bit. He put them all back. I couldn't bear to be in that room, and when my parents tried to force me I had a meltdown. I ended up in a children's psych ward over that Christmas. Of course, they had Christmas decorations everywhere to cheer up the kids, which only made me worse. It wasn't until after Christmas was over that I calmed down, and everyone ignored it until the following year, when I started to have panic attacks. Ever since then, Father Christmas has been a trigger for me. When I was eighteen I moved to the USA. Halloween and Thanksgiving are far more popular over there, so I didn't have to think about Christmas for so long. But every year, at the beginning of December, I took myself off traveling somewhere to avoid it.'

'But eventually you came back?'

'My mother wanted someone to take over the house. I decided that I would live in it after all. Cottonwood is fairly remote, so I could avoid most things to do with Christmas. Then I found out they were still running their accursed Christmas carnival.'

'So you shut it down?'

Nathan sighed. 'I was wrong. I wasn't thinking straight, and I abused the power that I had. I don't know if anyone will care, but I'm sorry.'

'I think they will care. And I think that in the true spirit of Christmas, they'll forgive you.'

'I don't need forgiveness. I just needed someone to know the truth. So they might understand. I talked through everything with Claudette—Mrs. Taylor—and she told me that if I explained what happened, it would make things easier to deal with.' He reached into his pocket and pulled out a tiny Father Christmas figurine.

'She also gave me this. She told me that by holding it in my hand, by facing it and realising it was just an image, I could slowly overcome my fear of it.'

'Has it worked?'

Nathan shrugged. 'So far, so good.'

'So you're finally coming to terms with it?'

'I'm doing my best. I feel numb to it rather than outright scared, but it does all leave a sour taste in my mouth. I want to enjoy it, but I don't think I can. All I can do is try to make peace with it so as not to ruin it for other people.'

'I'm proud of you, and very happy for you.'

Nathan grimaced. 'I never asked for this. I used to

enjoy Christmas just like everyone else, and that … evil man ruined it for me.'

He looked about to cry. Emily squeezed herself down on the sofa beside him and attempted to pat him on the shoulder. It was as close as she had ever been to him, but instead of the excitement she might once have expected, there was nothing. While his looks had once inspired a brief crush, it appeared to have been downgraded by the calamity of his personality.

'It's okay,' she said, feeling like a sister forgiving a wayward older brother she was welcoming back into the family after a spell out in the cold.

Nathan looked up, and even though his eyes were filled with tears, he smiled. 'You're dressed as a tree,' he said. 'It's very hard to talk about this to someone dressed as a tree.'

'It's symbolic,' Emily said, laughing. 'Symbolic of what brought me here. Would you like a mince pie? I have a few in the kitchen.'

Nathan nodded. 'That would be great,' he said. 'And, you know, I think my sugar levels are a bit low, so I could probably handle a hot chocolate too.'

34

COSTUMES

Emily was a little bleary-eyed and sore of throat for the Christmas carnival's opening ceremony at ten o'clock on Sunday morning. Nathan had declined her charitable offer to join her in the pub, insisting that he had to go home and belatedly put up a Christmas tree—another aspect of Mrs. Taylor's prescribed treatment, he told her—but most of the other locals had been there and much rowdiness had ensued. Emily's personal favorites had been Alan's babysitter Barbara standing on a table to belt out Gloria Gaynor's *I Will Survive* after several sherries too many, Skip attempting to take on the Bee Gees in a gravelly baritone, and Peter and Veronica's Grease duet, during which both of them had turned as red as tomatoes and downed tequilas to get through it, before sharing a tentative kiss at the end.

Walking up through the village, Emily met several locals also on their way up to the village hall and the main carnival site in its snow-covered car park. Not far from where a large inflatable snowman indicated the main entrance, she fell into step with Mrs. Taylor, who was carrying a pretty Yorkshire Terrier in a bag slung over her shoulder.

'Is this the elusive Cameron?' Emily asked, giving the dog a tentative pat on the head and receiving a low growl for her trouble.

Mrs. Taylor smiled. 'He didn't want to miss out. I might slip him a sausage on a stick if he's a good boy.'

'Thank you for talking to Nathan.'

Mrs. Taylor sighed. 'It was my pleasure. Honestly, in all the years I was working as a psychiatrist, I never came across a case quite like his. We had a long talk though, and I think he can be completely cured in time.'

'He told me about what happened when he was a child.'

'It must have been very traumatic, especially since no one believed him, and he was forced to go through the Christmas rigmarole year after year. I gather as a result he has a poor relationship with his mother, but that's something we're going to try to fix.'

'I hope so.'

'The biggest thing was having him face up to his fears. Gently, of course. You know, we actually managed to track down the man responsible for the robbery that Nathan witnessed. The man did his time and now lives on the other side of Exeter, married with a family. He works as a corrections officer dealing with juvenile criminals, and is very open to meeting with Nathan, both to apologise and try to allow Nathan some closure. He can't take back what happened, but he said he can try to make amends.'

'That's great. Is Nathan interested?'

'Very. He said he wants to get through this Christmas first, but will then meet up with the man after the New Year.'

'Do you think he'll come to the carnival?'

Mrs. Taylor shrugged. 'I'm not sure. He's very repentant about what he's done. Yesterday he filed a police report, detailing his supposed crimes. He's quite willing to pay for what he did, but I gather the police view was that the incidents were relatively minor in the great scheme of things. He called me afterwards to let me know how it went. I think the general gist was that if he made an effort to do something in the community then it would all get forgotten about.'

'That's good.'

Mrs. Taylor didn't answer. They had walked through on to the main site and she was staring straight ahead.

'Ooh, Cameron. What do I see over there? Sausages on sticks.' The dog gave a little bark, as though it had found the focus for its continued existence.

'I'll let you go,' Emily said. 'Hopefully I'll see you later.'

Mrs. Taylor waved goodbye, and Cameron gave Emily a parting growl. She turned left, making her way around the stalls one by one. Some were from outside the village, while others had been set up by local people. She came to Veronica's coffee and cake stall, where Veronica and Peter were sitting together on a bench, already in costume. With Veronica's extravagant golden dress next to Peter's green lycra skinsuit, they resembled a marigold fallen on its side.

'Bit cold, eh?' Veronica said. 'You want a coffee?'

Emily smiled. 'We'll work on how you greet customers when your training starts next year.'

Veronica brushed a strand of hair out of her face, fluttered her eyelids and said, 'Welcome, dear customer. Would you like to order one of our finest cups of coffee?' With a grin, she added, 'How was that?'

Beside her, Peter sniggered.

'Better,' Emily said. 'Somewhere in the middle would be ideal. But since you offered twice, yes, I'd very much like a coffee. And a cake with a lot of sugar in it, just to get the blood flowing.'

'Coming right up.'

Outside the village hall, a stage had been set up. Reverend Billingham introduced the local carol singing group, and a few minutes later the air filled with the lilting sound of traditional Christmas songs. Emily sat on a deck chair outside Veronica's stall to listen.

'Fourth from the left, back row, that's my mum,' Veronica said. 'She's got a lovely voice, eh.'

'She has,' Emily agreed. 'Why don't you join the group with her?'

Peter sniggered again, only to get an elbow in the ribs. 'What?' Veronica said. 'I have a great voice.'

'Not sure punk rock is what they're looking for.'

Veronica grinned. 'Peter and me are forming a band. He's on guitar and I'm the singer.'

'Really? You'll have to let me know when you play a show.'

Veronica looked at her watch. 'Four o'clock. We're gonna do *Last Christmas*.'

'Acoustic,' Peter said. 'We had our first practice last night, after we got back from the pub.'

'I'm good for most of the words,' Veronica said. 'If I forget any, I'll just freestyle.'

Emily laughed. 'I can't wait.'

∽

Karen arrived with David's family at about three o'clock. The minibus and its vanguard of Land Rovers was greeted with a hearty cheer as they disgorged several dozen visitors from nearby villages. Working in shifts, David and his six brothers—each dressed as a different dwarf—began a ferrying service to the Tesco car park just outside Exeter. By six o'clock, Cottonwood was nearly as crowded as Exeter city centre could be on a Saturday, with dozens of people lining the streets in anticipation of the parade.

Emily, worn out after an exciting day, hurried back to her holiday let to get her costume on. With the carnival procession due to start at seven, she had no time to waste in getting ready. Karen, already dressed as Maleficent, accompanied her, if only to offer moral support as Emily squeezed into the plastic tree costume.

It was quarter to seven when a knock came on the

door. Emily had managed to get one arm stuck, so Karen offered to answer it.

'Um, Emily, it's someone to see you,' Karen called from the hall. 'It's um, Elton John.'

'What?'

Emily stared as Elton John stepped into the living room. Huge, star-shaped glasses hid his eyes, while a blonde wig glittered under the ceiling light. An orange tracksuit had been hastily covered with glitter.

'Nathan?'

He shrugged. 'I just wondered … if you were going to the carnival, would you mind if I came along?'

'Absolutely not. That's an amazing costume.'

'Thanks. I wasn't keen on being recognised.'

'I'm sure you won't be. You might get a few looks, though. And you might get asked to do a karaoke turn-up at the village hall.'

Nathan shrugged. 'I know a couple of tunes, mostly the newer ones.'

Karen, standing behind him, laughed. 'I didn't think anyone knew those.'

'Oh, they're missing out,' Nathan said. 'I produced the album before his current one. Elton's like a fine wine. He'll only keep getting better.'

Behind him, Karen mouthed, 'Is he being serious?' to which Emily just shrugged.

'It might be a bit late notice for this year, but I might be able to get him to come down next year,' Nathan said. 'Maybe play a couple of tunes.' He shrugged. 'If the parish council agrees to it.'

'I thought you were the parish council.'

Nathan shook his head. 'I've decided to resign. It's probably for the best.'

Karen tapped her wrist. 'Well, I think we'd better get going, otherwise we'll miss the start. If, of course, you're ready.'

Emily gave the tree suit one last tug and finally managed to slip her hand past the section that was sticking.

'Right,' she said. 'Let's do this.'

~

Outside, Cottonwood appeared to have doubled in size. At least a hundred people wore costumes of one kind or another, everything from homemade fairies and elves to shop-bought snowman outfits, twin-person reindeer suits, and even one person dressed as a giant star. There were also several processional floats, including one pulled behind Alan's tractor which was a hilariously out of season seashore scene with half a dozen children dressed as fish and crabs even as the snow gently fell around him.

Again, Reverend Billingham, himself dressed as a motorcycle stuntman, stepped up to a microphone set up outside the Inn on the Green to introduce the carnival.

'After a couple of fallow years, we're back in full swing here in Cottonwood,' he said to a series of cheers. 'I'd like to give a big thanks to the organisers, in particularly to Emily Wilson from up in Birchtide, whose tireless work here managed to get us back into the spirit of things. Emily, where are you? Can you come and have a word, please?'

Emily felt her cheeks redden. She hadn't expected to have to say something, but as people spotted her and waved her forward, she realised she had no choice. Awkwardly struggling through the snow, she made her way over to the microphone and took it from Reverend Billingham, who had begun to laugh uncontrollably at her costume.

'Thank you, everyone, for coming,' Emily said. 'This was really a group effort. When I came here only a couple of weeks ago, what struck me most was how kind and welcoming the local people were to me. I came here with a few issues of my own, and I was made to feel welcome and part of a family. So, thank you all.' She paused as people began to clap. 'I came here because I lost my grandmother back in October. She was everything to me, and without her, I didn't know what to do. I lost all grip on who I was and where I was going in life. Thanks to the people I've met here in Cottonwood, I'm looking forward to the future with a renewed optimism. For those of you who don't know, my grandmother was Elaine Wilson, owner of Elaine's Teahouse, over in Birchtide. If anyone finds themselves passing over the next few months, stop in and say hi. Tell me you were here and you'll get a drink and cake on the house.'

The crowd cheered even louder. Emily caught sight of Karen in the crowd, giving her a quizzical expression. She smiled and nodded.

'And now, I'll hand you back to someone who's far better at speaking in public than me, and, you know, not distractingly dressed as a tree. Everyone … thanks for coming, and enjoy the carnival.'

Another cheer rose as Emily passed the microphone back to Ted and made her way over to where Karen was waiting.

'So, is it official? You're going to open up Elaine's place again?'

Emily nodded. 'Only it's not Elaine's place anymore. It's mine.'

Karen gave her an awkward hug. 'I'm so glad. Birchtide just wouldn't be the same without it.'

'It won't be quite the same as before,' Emily said. 'I have a few plans and ideas I'd like to try.'

'Well, at the grand reopening, I'll be first in line.'

Emily laughed. 'I'd expect nothing else. Come on, let's go grab some popcorn and a drink before they start the procession.'

35

AFTERWARD

A BRIGHT BLUE SKY GREETED EMILY ON HER return to Birchtide. A couple of days of warmth had begun to melt off the lying snow, but another heavy snowfall was due on Christmas Eve, so Emily knew she had to get going over to Karen's before then.

With great reluctance, she had turned down an offer from Alan to have Christmas dinner at Rowe Farm, deciding instead to give Karen some moral support at David's for a few days. She would certainly have liked to be a fly on the wall; after all, Alan had also invited Nathan, Mrs. Taylor, Skip, and both Peter and Veronica's entire families. Alan, who had promised to stop by the teahouse sometime in early January, would surely give her a complete talk through.

Like the aging of a fine wine, her feelings for the farmer had taken some time to develop. Whenever she thought about Nathan now, she found herself smiling at his awkwardness and feeling a sense of relief that he had found some kind of closure.

When she thought of Alan, however, things seemed a little different.

She thought of his welcoming kitchen with its natural warmth, and off the smiles of the children so eager to see her again. She imagined relaxing walks in the fields with a cool, clear winter sky overhead, and of quiet evenings sitting around his open fire, mulling over the events of the day.

And most of all, she thought of his kind, resilient smile, and the unfaltering brightness of his eyes. The eyes of a man who had been through so much, the eyes of man who deserved to find happiness and peace.

She was looking forward to seeing him, so much that the idea of it gave her a little tingle in the stomach. She had already sent him an email suggesting an arrangement to supply milk for her business. His reply had come so quickly it was almost as though he'd been waiting for it, and it gave them a reason to meet again early in the new year. There had been something latent there for sure, hidden perhaps behind more serious events, but now that the roads were clear, other developments were free to happen. Emily was putting no pressure on it, however. She had her own priorities now, which would take up much of her time.

One of them was hiring some new staff.

As she walked up the path to the teahouse entrance, she saw the signboard she had placed outside still stood where she had left it, underneath the porch roof. A swirling text surrounded by a flower design announced:

ELAINE & EMILY'S
GRAND REOPENING
JANUARY 1ˢᵗ

Pinned to the chalkboard were dozens of messages of support, plastic flowers, even a teddy bear.

She smiled.

It would go well, she was sure. Particularly with Veronica to help her. For the first month at least, after which Veronica would be coming every Monday, to learn more about running a business and dealing with customers. Emily had put it to Veronica that she affiliate her little shop in Cottonwood with the teahouse, and the girl had jumped at the chance. Emily required a certain standard, so Veronica would need to be put through her paces, and Emily would have to visit Cottonwood frequently to ensure her standards were being met. Veronica, however, had been so excited she had even offered to cut her hair, although Emily had vehemently refused.

'You've got to be you,' she said. 'Customers will see through an act in a second. That's what my grandmother always said.'

She put her suitcase down outside the door and fumbled in her pocket for her key. Over the door the sign read, "Elaine's Teahouse". Emily had already ordered a replacement, to add her own name. It should be arriving just after Christmas.

The hard work began now, but it was a challenge Emily felt ready for. She unlocked the door and let herself inside.

'I'm back,' she said, then added, 'I'm home.'

And meant it.

END

ABOUT THE AUTHOR

CP Ward loves writing Christmas books. This is his third attempt, after last year's well-received *I'm Glad I Found you this Christmas* and *We'll Have a Wonderful Cornish Christmas* earlier this year. There will certainly be more…

CP Ward would love to hear from you:
chrisward@amillionmilesfromanywhere.net

Printed by Amazon Italia Logistica S.r.l.
Torrazza Piemonte (TO), Italy